GARBAGE

Also by Stephen Dixon
NO RELIEF (story collection), 1976
WORK (novel), 1977
TOO LATE (novel), 1978
QUITE CONTRARY (story collection), 1979
14 STORIES (story collection), 1980
MOVIES (story collection), 1983
TIME TO GO (story collection), 1984
FALL & RISE (novel), 1985

A novel by
Stephen Dixon

CANE HILL PRESS

Part of this novel appeared in slightly different form in *Confrontation;* the author and the publisher extend their thanks.

Library of Congress Catalog Number 87-70931
Printed in the United States of America
   First Edition
ISBN No. 0-943433-00-2

Cover photograph by John R. Humphreys
Cover design by Larry Zirlin
Calligraphy by Joy Schleh

Published by
Cane Hill Press
225 Varick Street
New York, New York 10014

 Produced at The Print Center., Inc., 225 Varick St., New York, NY 10014, a non-profit facility for literary and arts-related publications. (212) 206-8465

To Andrew Rock and Warren Jay Hecht
who called

Two men come in and sit at the bar. I say "How you doing, fellas, what'll it be?"

"What are you, about to close?" the stocky one says.

"No, it's just empty for a change. Still want to stay?"

"Sure. Beers. Whatever you got."

"I have draft, I have bottles. Domestic and imported in both."

"Two draft whatever kind you want. We're in no rush."

"Got you."

I draw the beer and give it to them, ring up the tab and set it down between them.

"You Shaney?" the stocky one says.

"That's right."

"You're the owner of this bar."

"Owner and bartender both."

"Well lookit, Shaney, you pour a good beer. Nice head on it. You don't often get a head on beer anymore at bars and you got a beaut on yours. That's good."

"It's the way you draw the beer that gives it the head. I can almost make the head any size I want."

"Yeah, how so?"

"You hold the glass under the spout a certain way, at a forty-five degree angle, like this." I take a glass from the sink rack and hold it at the forty-five degree angle in front of them. "Then when—"

"Put it under the tap for real and pour yourself one on us."

"No thanks. I have only one drink a day and that's a stiff belt at the end of the evening after I close."

"Smart man. Won't drink more yourself because you know what it does to you. That's unusual for a bartender."

"Not so much when he owns the place."

"But you were saying about pouring your beer, Shaney?"

"How'd you know my name by the way?"

"Oh, a pal of ours comes in here and says it's a good spot for a sandwich and beer and your name's Shaney, that's all."

"What's his name?"

"Dave is it?" he asks the thinner man.

"Dave. I don't know his last."

"Dave?" I say. "I don't think I know a Dave, at least not well enough to say I know the name right away."

"He used to come in," the stocky one says "and maybe he still does. And we were around the neighborhood, doing some late work here—we're salesmen—and I said there's where Dave mentioned that bar and the owner's name is Shaney. If your name was John or Jim I wouldn't've remembered it."

"That's what he told me," the thinner man says. "The part about there's where you are."

"But about getting the good head on the beer. Show me carefully so I can tell my other bartender friends who don't know about it."

"I'm sure they all do, if they've been tending bar for more than a week. It's not a new trick."

"No, you'd be surprised. Most of them say it's the beer today that won't make a good head. So it'll be my kind of service to them, you could say, because I know it should bring in more customers. Every drinker likes a big head on his beer, one he can wipe off his lips."

"You actually want to know?"

"Why, do I sound like I'm kidding you?"

"In a way."

"I'm not, honestly. Go ahead, show me."

"You hold the glass like this, pull down the tap and let the beer out of it into the glass. Then when the beer's about an inch and a half from the top, you pop the tap handle to its nonpouring position same time you straighten the glass under the spout and catch the beer that's still coming out. Of course you can't be at the end of your keg and you have to have enough pressure in the pipes and the beer's got to be a certain temperature—forty-two degrees is the best. Not too warm or too cold.''

"Now I know. By the way, Shaney—"

"You want another beer? I'm not pushing, but you finished yours so fast.''

"No thanks. It'll get me fat.''

"On the house. Always a free one after the first one for a new customer who looks like he might drop in again, and you're under no obligation to take more than a sip from it.''

"Okay, what the hell. Give me another.''

"Me too,'' the thinner man says "not that I'm asking for it on the house. He's having one, I'm going to too.'' He drains his glass and gives me it.

"Listen,'' I say "you're a new customer too.''

I get two glasses out of the refrigerator and draw them another beer each.

"It also helps to have a fresh chilled glass to get that head,'' I say, giving them their beers.

"By the way, Shaney,'' the stocky one says "who does your trash pickup?''

"My garbage? What's that to you? I'm curious.''

"You see, we also represent a company that does garbage pickup and they'd like to pick up for you. Stovin Private Carting Service.''

"Never heard of it. Eco Carting does mine. They're good and reliable and come in the worst of storms, so I'm sorry but I can't.''

"Well we're new around here, though very modern and organized, and would like to pick up for you instead of Eco. How about it?''

"I told you, I'd like to. But I don't even have that much garbage for one carter.''

"If you don't let us cart for you there might be heavy trouble with Stovin's when I tell them. They want to cart all the business garbage in the area—at least all the bars around here and grocery stores. Kelly's Bar just signed with us and he was being picked up by Eco before."

"Look, what are you guys? You musclemen, that it? Well I like Eco, been with them for years, and that's that, okay? So get lost."

"You want a broken window, Shaney?"

"Don't start with me. Two of you, I'll still give you a busted head each."

"And don't give us that tough crap talk either."

"He's right," the thinner man says. "Don't be smart, Shaney. Better for your health. Better for all our healths, because if we start having it out, everybody's going to get hurt."

"My health is good. Don't threaten me. Do, I can call the police."

"You just do that," the stocky one says. "Just do. You'll not only have broken windows, you'll have a burnt-out bar. Now what do you say? Our rates may be a little higher than Eco. But we're a very good carting service, very reliable too. Sun or rain, and if any other carter tries to move in on you, just tell us and we'll deal with them for you."

"I don't need any protection from anyone but you."

"Get Eco to protect you then."

"They don't do that. They're an honest carter."

"So are we. Except we need the business now, a lot of business, as we invested heavily in trucks and stuff and don't want to stay in debt. So I'll ask you a last time. You changing over to us?"

"Just a matter of curiosity, what are your rates?"

"Sixty a month."

"You crazy? Eco's is thirty-five."

"I said we're a little higher. But it'll be worth it. We pick up five mornings a week."

"Eco does it every morning but Monday."

6

"I'm telling you what we do, not Eco. Maybe we can pick up more trash for you than them—how about that?"

"They take away everything I put on the street. And if it's something like an old sink that's too heavy for me, they come right inside."

"Hey, I'm tired of talking. You in with us or not?"

"All I want is for you to get out of here, all right? Don't worry about paying." I grab the tab and tear it up and throw it on the floor. "There. Now just get out."

"I'd like some kind of answer for my company."

"You don't know what to tell them?"

"Don't get too excited with your words, Shaney. Be nice, stay calm. Let my bosses know through me you're both those ways. That's the minimum I can do for you for your foam lesson and free beers. If I were you I'd tell me to tell them you're thinking about it. That way you have time."

"Time for what?"

"For thinking about it."

"I'm thinking about it then. That make you feel better?"

"Good man." He puts a ten dollar bill on the bar and leaves with the other man. I yell "You paid too goddamn much, fella," as they go through the door.

I call Kelly and tell him what just happened and ask if he really did switch from Eco to Stovin.

"I had to, Shaney. I know those bums. They throw a brick through your window one night, next night they drop a stink-bomb when customers are around and so on. Next thing you know your life and trade aren't worth a dime. It's protection money you're paying them, and with your temper, maybe protecting them from you. They also cart. So you get less carting, so what? Stick what they don't pick up in the corner trash can, but at least you'll be alive."

"What do you know what happens if you go to the police?"

"That I don't advise and don't tell Stovin's you asked me about it. But go, and bricks, bombings, I hear everything but jet fighters can come down on you at one time. Give them the sixty and forget about it."

I don't know what to do. Maybe they'll give up on me now knowing I'm absolutely against them carting for me and they'd be better spending their time trying to change the mind of another storeowner who's an easier mark. I'll just take a wait-and-see attitude without maybe stirring up more trouble with them by calling the police.

Same two men come in two nights later and sit at the bar. The stocky one says "Hi, Shaney."

The thinner one says "How you doing tonight, Shaney?"

A young couple, almost teenagers—I didn't check their ID's because business isn't so good and they looked over the minimum age—are sitting at the other end of the bar. I just finished giving them a couple more tequila sunrises and I go over to the men.

"Those two down there," the stocky man says. "They're not junior undercovers, are they?"

"What's your name?"

"Why you want to know?"

"You know mine, I want to know both of yours. I don't see why that should be a problem, and it'll be easier for me to speak."

"I'm Pete, he's Turner. But those kids down there."

"Why would they be?"

"Or the fellows at the table in back. They look it."

"No, nobody here's anything but plain customers, which I wish you guys were too."

"We will be if you do what we ask you to and not what we don't like. You called Kelly, didn't you?"

"No."

"Kelly told us. He didn't volunteer so don't go getting back at him. But we knew you'd call him so we called him ourselves today and first he said no and when we said you already told us you called him, he said yes you did. He advised you right, didn't he?"

"He advised me to let you cart my garbage."

8

"And you're taking his advice, right?"

"No, I don't think so. I don't want to be protected."

"Talk lower."

"I can't afford sixty, that's another thing. It's too much."

"If we made a special deal of fifty for you, but nothing less, you'd do it, right?"

"Let me think about it."

"Think about it now. We don't want any more stalling."

"I need time to think. I don't make money decisions quickly."

"I said think about it now. Get us some beers just to make it seem more like we're here for pleasure and not so much hard business."

I start drawing them their beers.

"And put a real big head on those, Shaney, just like the other night."

I give them the beers with a big head. Pete puts a ten on the bar. "Keep it. See—already you're twenty dollars ahead with us. So consider the first month as only being thirty dollars for our services, five less than what you pay Eco, if you go with the fifty we'll charge you a month. Now what do you say? I can only give you three more minutes of thinking time. Things are picking up for us around here, so we're very busy."

"How would I explain to Eco?"

"Just say you felt it better going with us because we gave you a better deal."

"Fifteen dollars more a month is better with one less pickup day?"

"That you don't tell him."

"Suppose he says what was the deal so he can maybe meet it?"

"You say you already made up your mind."

"But I know Eco personally. George Ecomolos. He comes in for beers every now and then. I know his garbage guys. They've been with him for ten to twenty years and I give them free shots and a sandwich every now and then. They're nice guys—Eco himself a nice guy too. No, I can't do it."

"Don't worry. Once you stop paying Eco to cart for you, he won't come in to drink again."

"I said I can't, that's it. You want trouble, well all right, you're talking to the guy who can give it. Big deal. Bust a window of mine out or throw a bomb in whatever it's made of—explosives, fire—but you'll wind up in more trouble than me. Believe me, much more."

"Don't be silly—we can't be. Now is it no or yes? Just sign your fate with a single word, Shaney. Yes or the other?"

"No, damn you. I said no."

"Okay, pal. See you."

"Bye bye, Shaney," Turner says.

They get up to go.

"Wait," I say when they're almost out the door.

"Okay for a quick change of mind," Pete says. "As I said, we're very busy."

"No, forget it. I almost changed it but I can't. I'll take my chances. I'm also calling the police."

"You're getting so silly it's ridiculous."

"Remember, these people are my witnesses. They saw you in here."

"Saw what?" the young man at the bar says.

"You going to involve these nice kids, Shaney? Besides, they seem too young to even be drinking. You could lose your license."

"I'm nineteen," the young man says "and she's legal age too."

"No, you're right," I say to Pete "I'm leaving them out of it. I'll do it all on my own. My father had a bar before me, did you know that?"

"Not interested," Pete says.

"Hey bartender," one of the men at the back table yells "bring us another pitcher of beer."

"And my grandfather on my mother's side before him and some great-uncles too. They were all tough and I'm tough, tough as you guys, that you better believe. Maybe tougher because it's for so long inherited.''

''I'm sure of it, Shaney. I'm shivering in my jeans. And get your old man and hundred-year-old uncles to stand up with you.'' They leave.

''What was that all about?'' the young woman says.

''Something. But if you don't mind I'd like you both to go now, last round on the house, but come in again when I'm not so shaken up.''

They leave. I get the back table a pitcher of beer and fresh glasses and call the police.

Two detectives come later that night. One says ''We'll keep someone out front tonight if you want. We'd also like to hook up a recorder under the bar with a foot pedal on it, just in case they come in again, so we can get them on tape. Unless they threaten you when you've witnesses or you get it recorded, it's impossible to prove who's telling the truth. Customers in back know anything?''

''They heard us arguing maybe, but didn't know what it was or were too stewed to. And I don't want recorders, just police protection. But I swear to you, those same two come in again when you're not around, then no questions or anything I'm going to hit them over the head with my club.''

''Don't hit anyone. Let us do the hitting for you if it has to come to that.''

''I want them to know I mean business.''

''So they'll know, so what—you want to get yourself killed? Maybe they won't come back. Sometimes it's all words and no deed with them and they don't even work for who they say they do but just want the money on the spot, in cash. We'll check in with Stovin's tomorrow early. For now what do you say to kicking those clowns out and closing up for some rest?''

''I'm closing regular time only—nothing's making me do otherwise. I don't want those punks thinking they scared me even a half hour out of my place.''

I close at three, clean the bar, refill the stock and put the garbage out on the street and have my double shot of scotch and beer chaser and lock up the place. A police car's parked across the street. I go over to it and the man inside says he's been assigned to the post for the night. I walk home. My phone's ringing when I unlock the door.

"Shaney my love," Pete says "what's been keeping you? Boy, was that stupid of you calling in the law. Stupid, stupid— what could you have been thinking of? Anyway, they can't stay there forever—even cops got to make pee. When they finally give up the watch as unproductive we might dynamite the joint with you in it or not—we haven't as yet quite decided. You still don't want us to work for you though, right?"

"Right."

"Last time I can be talking to you like this. No more polite social teas and cutesy-pie chats from me, so also don't bother with taps and tapes. Now once more—make up our minds. We haul a hell of a great barrel of trash."

"No thanks."

"Oh well. Maybe you'll be a good lesson for some other possible dope," and he hangs up.

I call the police and tell them I want a tap on my home and business phones. Next day I awake the same time I do every morning and get set for work. I'll be in at nine-thirty and open by ten and work to the end. I do that seven days a week. Been doing it for eighteen years straight, not one day off for vacation or being sick even when I had a hundred and three fever. I got this bar from my father. He got it from his father-in-law, though it was a different bar then, same name, in another part of town. It never made enough to support more than one family and it could probably just barely do that now. My father when I worked for him often warned me "Never give in to extortion ever. Do it once, they'll be on you always. They'll next want you to buy your liquor from them, then the mixers, then the records to rent for your machine. Then everything, even the bar coasters and lightbulbs. Before you know it they'll own a good piece of the place and you'll be working for them. Say no sir from the start. They'll threaten but the chances are they won't come through. And keep in contact with the police on this, though do what you can on your own without hurting yourself, since less the police have to do with the bar the better. If the police want a little palming for extra protecting and investigating, don't give them anything but food and booze or soon they'll be robbing you blind too. They still insist and you need them, go higher up till you get results. That'll all happen a few times in your barowning life and if you ride it out, you've won. You give in just once, you're sunk. You might as well stand on the other side of your bar and drink your business away, since that's what'll happen to it: straight down the drain.''

Next morning around eleven two detectives come in, dressed like truckers, and tell me the Stovin company denied ever even hearing of my bar. ''They say they got all the garbage they can handle now and which the city will allow them to dump and they've nobody working for them named Turner or Pete. They let us look through their recent financial and employment records, which they didn't have to, and they seem to be as honest a private carter as one could be without allowing us a look at their original books. If you don't mind we'll pretend to be your customers on and off for a week, though to make it look realer you'll have to put out for our food and an occasional rye and beer.''

''Fine with me.''

''Department will reimburse you for everything we eat.''

''Even better, as it'll at least guarantee me a couple of steady customers all week.''

Two teams of policemen hang around on eight-hour shifts apiece, mostly playing cards and studying for college exams or watching the back TV. I get no attempted anything or threatening phone call. At the end of the week one of the policemen says ''We'll only observe the bar from the outside now. Nothing much, as it doesn't look like anything will happen: a passing car or cop on the beat. We'll keep the tap in, not to listen but to record your calls.''

''What should I do if they march in here again?''

"Phone us if you can, though God knows what I'd do if I were you. Probably, for just the fifteen bucks more a month, I would've let them have my garbage, even if I only half believed they'd hit on me or my place. Now that you came to us, if what you say is on the level, they wouldn't do your garbage for ten times the amount and maybe got scared away. We'll see. Fortunately, you don't have a wife and kids. You did, they'd have threatened them to you and I bet you would've given in the first day."

"My dad never did and I don't think I would've also, but then how am I to know?"

"Your father's times, those were different. People mostly murdered each other in their sleep, not out on the street. Today everyone's got his homemade bomb and seven types of rifles and handguns. Maybe you should get one yourself. You'd be entitled to, I'd think, what with all those threats."

Next morning I go to police headquarters. Person in charge of gun licensing says "You've got to produce a definite witness who saw or heard your life or business being threatened or you to prove at least twice this year where your bar got robbed. Because without someone taking the chance under oath of standing up for you and then going to jail himself if it turns out he lied, half the city would be carrying concealed revolvers and shooting off their testicles and toes."

I probably could find someone to lie for me for a dozen free drinks, but then I'd be into another person for something else. Besides, I'm an old club man—I know how to swing one and knock out a troublemaker with one quick blow without breaking his skull. If a man came in with a gun and I also had one, I'd probably reach for it and blow out the window instead of his brains and then he'd pop me away for sure. I also don't think I could live with myself if I killed anyone—I just want to help whoever's threatening me to forever get lost.

Business is the same as usual the next week: not so good. Police check in with me every night personally and once a day by phone.

14

"How's it going?"

"Nothing's happened if that's what you mean."

"Don't complain."

"I'm not," but by this time they've usually already hung up.

Once when a policeman says "How's it going?" I say "Suppose some punk had a gun to my neck right now and told me to say nothing's happening, how would you know?"

"Does one?"

"If anyone did, you think he'd let me tell you?"

"Honestly now—no games. If anyone does have a gun on you, he doesn't have to know who you're actually talking to or your joking style, so say very naturally to me 'I'm only fooling, Luke—I'll take five kegs of bock and three normal ale, but this time make it cheap.'"

"Nobody does."

"Then why frighten me like that? Stay loose."

One night, week after I went for the gun license, a customer I never saw before comes in, has a mug of beer and two hard-boiled eggs, says goodnight and leaves. On the bar napkin is a message written on it under his half-dollar tip: "Shaney, dear. Your place is getting effaced tonight. Bet you couldn't wait. Sorry, sweet. Love, Pete."

I call the police. They come with sirens on and in droves, order me to close for the night, shut all the lights and we sit in an unmarked van across the street waiting for anyone suspicious to stop in front of the bar with something that could have inside it a firebomb or can of gasoline. Nobody stops for anything except the bakery driver, who at daybreak leaves against my door his daily bag of breadloafs and rolls.

Hour later one of the three policemen in the van says "Nothing's getting effaced today and I'm starving, so what do you guys say?" and we go into the bar for coffee and eggs I'll make and some of those rolls. A few minutes later the phone rings.

"So there you are," my landlady at home says. "I've been calling and calling and getting more worried every second and already was accepting the fate you were so charred you didn't leave a single trace."

"What are you talking about?"

"Your apartment early this morning. The fire, where all your rooms except the toilet were almost altogether destroyed. Thank heavens we saved the rest of the building and our lives because your nextdoor neighbors had the foresight to put in smoke alarms. The fire marshal's right beside me and he—"

"Let me speak to him," I hear a man say.

"He wants to know if you left something cooking on your stove or can remember a cigarette in your ashtray or lit match."

"Mr. Fleet?" a man says on the phone.

"Listen," I say to him. "I left for work almost twenty-four hours ago. You think it would've taken that long or whatever hours it was to start a fire if I ever had the dumbness to leave anything cooking there? Well I don't have the dumbness for that and gave up smoking a dozen years ago and throwing away lit matches without watching where they dropped about twenty years before that and nobody but me and my landlady who has the keys and a plumber or two has been in my apartment for five years. That fire was deliberately done by some company that's trying to steamroll me to doing something I don't want to do and if you want to talk to anyone about it, come over here and speak to the police."

"You stay there—someone will watch your apartment—and I'll be right over."

"Goddammit I'm mad," I yell, slamming down the phone. I throw the eggs on, scoop out the shells from the yolks because I threw them on so fast and then slice the rolls so quick I sliver my hands twice and my blood sizzles on the grill. "I'm mad, those bastards," and I throw the spatula against the wall and punch my palm till it hurts.

"You want us to take over the stove?" one of the policemen says.

The marshal comes in while we're sitting around a table eating and I say "Want breakfast? I know I can't touch mine," and he says "No, I go home for dinner right after this—I got the moon shift, lucky me. But what've you guys got that's so hot?" and a policeman shows him the note the man left last night.

"This spit-stained napkin's supposed to prove something to me?"

"Well I didn't write it," I say. "Besides, you don't believe me, the hell with you—I got to see my apartment."

"Whoa, whoa. Lookit, not that I'm saying what I'm going to say happened or even implying you were any way in the wrong. But knowledgeably speaking, anyone could have written this napkin for you so you could get your insurance company, we'll say, to think your apartment fire wasn't paid for or invited by you."

"I don't have apartment insurance. If I burned anything down it would be this unprofitable bar, but without first calling the police there'll be a fire, though maybe even there you think that's another ruse. Besides which I never hurt anyone except some dumb—wait a minute. You see a parrot in the apartment?"

"A statue of one?"

"Real."

"No."

"No parrot, live or dead or anything looking like a bird?"

"No, why, you had one?"

"Would I be asking? Maybe she flew away. I always kept the window open a little so she could get fresh air, though when it really matters to them, animals can squeeze out of anywheres. But I had my windows wide open last summer and she never flew away yet. And plenty of times had the chance, having picked open the latch with her beak or I let her free to fly and crap all over the place and me because I suddenly couldn't see her caged, though a fire's another thing."

"It was a pretty serious one, so your bird's body could have gotten hid under the debris."

"I'll just have to hope she flew away and someone caught her

17

before she froze. But I never hurt anyone I was saying except some bum who was hurting someone else in my bar and wouldn't stop or with his big mouth causing all my customers to flee, and then I only hurt his feelings some if he still wouldn't go. Showed him the club and even used it on him light at times when he tried to rush me with a knife. Another thing: think I'd be fool enough to knock out the place I've lived in for fifteen years? And which to duplicate somewhere else, or even the same one, because they can charge me what they want once I'm burnt out and they put it back in shape—forget the cost to my soul if even one smelly puppy goes up in smoke because of me—I'd have to shell out three times the rent I now pay? Don't be stupid."

"And don't shoot off your mouth like that to me."

"I don't deserve to? Being accused by you, threatened by others, my apartment burnt out, parrot gone, a hotel to go to now—you're going to put me up?"

"Easy, fellas," a policeman says.

"Then tell him to lay off. I've enough troubles."

"Lookit," the marshal says. "I know you've a good rep in your apartment building. Quiet and courteous and Mr. Joe Concerned Dogooder Citizen when you've the time to and so forth."

"Oh please. Stop chopping and packaging the bullcrap."

"That's what she said—your landlady and other tenants. And your record for arson or suspected with my department and your whole family line of bar licenses is bloodbank clean. I checked. But I have to think of every possibility what started the fire—that's my job."

"Go to Stovin's then—you with these men. Show them the note. Don't be afraid. Show them it and say point blank they wrote it and watch their faces lie in their protests."

"All we can do is go there, if these officers are willing, and question them about your charges and see what's what. I'm sure though that if anyone was intimidating you for the reasons you said, then with that fire he's stopped."

18

The policemen and marshal go. I'm exhausted and because I never could get anyone to work for me steady, being every mopman and bartender I had the past few years turned out to be the worst sort of loafer, drunk or thief or all three, I close up for the first time in my barowning life when there's still daylight out, other than for my mother's funeral. A policeman's to stay in front of my place guarding it but I don't see one. Hell, let Stovin's burn down the bar. At least I'll get insurance on it, though I make sure to take all the cash I keep under the counter for the next day's change and things.

I go home. Home's a burnt-out two rooms but a john which still works. I take a last pee in it, retrieve what I can which isn't much but shaving and tooth-cleaning things and a pure pewter beer mug of my grandfather's for a sausage-eating contest he won a hundred years ago and which is almost still too hot to touch, and give a last look around for the parrot before I choke to death. I find her half dug in by her beak and claws to my one floor plant. Sara wasn't originally mine but a gift, though her owner said "on loan," in lieu of six months of unpaid bar bills. But I grew fond of her and she of me and I liked to talk to her when I got home from work or Sundays when I couldn't by law open the bar till noon. "Got a match?" she'd say from the previous owner every time I walked in the door and I'd say, hanging up my coat, "Sara, how you doing? Don't you know by now I don't smoke?"·

"No match?"

"No ma'am, I told you, I no smoke."

"No ma'am I no got a match."

"So now you no smoke."

"No smoke?"

"You and I no smoke."

"I so now you no smoke got a match?" back to me or something and so on till we somehow wound up at the beginning and then I'd stop.

I pull out the plant, put Sara in the hole and cover her with earth, feel sad about it, stick a pen up in the pot as a headstone, finally let a few tears go for the loss of my place and mate, wash the singed feathers and fronds and blood and smell off my hands and leave.

A fireman's outside my door drinking coffee when he wasn't there before and says "Nobody's supposed to be in there and what do you have in that bag?" and I say "It's all right, I'm family."

I say goodbye to the landlady, check into a hotel nearby and sleep a few hours and reopen the bar, since I've nothing else to do and it's not only my livelihood but where I see just about every social contact I know. Same woman in regular clothes is still in a private car in front of my bar and drives away talking into a two-way the moment I unlock the door, so I guess she was my police guard.

The marshal calls next day and says "We've no proof whatsoever that Stovin's had anything to do with your fire. Maybe it was someone in your apartment building who wanted you moved out or just a bar customer with a grudge."

"And the police, what do they think?"

"Agree a hundred percent. But they did tell me to tell you, as they're very busy today and knew I'd call, that they've removed the taps on your phones."

"The one on my home phone wasn't too tough to remove, was it?"

"I'm fire, they're police, so I wouldn't know."

"Listen. You're ever around the bar for a drink, drop in."

"I've wives to slide home to, pal, but thanks."

"Free, on me, all you can guzzle and eat, because you've been all right."

"Different story then. I might drop by tonight."

"I once wanted to be a fireman," I tell him that evening. "But after whiffing for the first time what an apartment fire was like and seeing my poor bird turned into a crow, I'm glad I followed the family tradition of owning a losing bar."

"My father and only older brother died in the same fire once," he says. "Yeah, after that happened they made a law saying no two family of the same members, of the same immediate, brother-in-laws and cousins excluded—you know what I mean."

"Yes."

"Can serve in the same fire station or even district. We're famous as a name in fires. It's called the Dibbeny Law which is our name and is now almost coastwide."

"Must've been some blow to you, losing both."

"It killed me. It was arson." He's now crying. "Maybe the only good thing it did was get me out of the navy as a hardship case at the start of my hitch to support my mother and brother's kids. I'm still trying to find the guy who did it twenty years later, but of course know that's crazy, which is only between you and me."

"Which leads me—mind if we talk some more about it?"

"Go on. I told you, I'm really dead."

"What are the chances of finding the ones who burnt me?"

"If they're pros, zero. If they're not, give it ten percent. Even me, who's a crackerjack investigator for eight years now and took no bribes yet to digress me, my success story is no better than sixteen point five percent and most of those were jealous rage ones, so easy."

He gets sloshed and breaks down at the bar again but this time doesn't recover and starts coughing like I never heard anyone and muttering "Brudder, fudder—ah rats, oh crap, tap me again, Shaney, zap zap," and I have to pry the glass out of his hand and put him in back to rest and call his sons to pick him up.

"He's not supposed to drink," one of the sons says as they walk Dibbeny out. "Because of all the smoke he ingested over the years his insides got messed and changed and maybe his brains, so don't do us any more favors by serving him, you hear?"

"Got you, son."

Next afternoon an envelope's dropped through the bar's mail slot. No stamp, just my address and initials on it, and inside a typewritten note saying "From Shaney to Shaney: written on my typewriter as a reminder night before I had a bosomy friend set fire to my apartment: answer phone!"

Phone rings right then. There's a phonebooth across the street but nobody's in it. I lift the receiver.

"It's Pete, sweetie, how's tricks?"

"I was wondering when."

"Today, sweetie, today. But no time for amenities. I just want to direct and you listen and act."

"I don't know what your amenities means."

"Social intercourse. Nice blab-blab. 'How's you? What's new? Kill a gay? Fornicate today?' But you haven't a customer now, as that's not how it was planned, so don't use that as an excuse you can't do the following what I'm about to say."

"I want to see you guys about my fire."

"What it is is this. Go with a thousand dollars—I know you can get it from your bank in ten minutes, and there's no line right now—to a phonebooth on Second and Prescott. You'll find a strip of thick adhesive tape taped under the phone shelf. Stick the thousand, which you'll have stuck in an envelope to that tape, and fly back to your bar and make yourself an assuager sooner than you're used to. The tape's quite gummy so don't worry about bringing your own tape or your envelope falling off unless it's made of concrete. Bills to be large, naturally aged, of our nationality and denomination, ten of them to be precise, so decide what kind that is on your way to the bank. Do this now. Lock up, go. We're watching you. Call in the cops and next time it'll be two thousand we ask for and each time you bring cops in and stall us, a thousand more. But you're not getting away from us till your dues are paid. We let one get by like you the rest might think 'Hey, that's the way!' and next there could be open rebellion in the dumps and streets and then where would the free enterprise and great civilization system be? We're being extremely lenient with you and you're getting off light, though no other storeowner will, in case they ask you. That thousand you pay, or two thousand if you delay, is what we'll deem the termination of our garbage contract which we think you thought was finished with just one charred apartment," and he hangs up.

I have my drink now, another one, chase them with ale, chase that with another scotch, man comes in and I grab my club and say "You from Stovin's?" and he says "No, just want a beer," and I say "Well go, closed, I'm sorry but I'm in no kind of mood to serve," and he goes and I call Stovin's and say "This is Shaney Fleet please, let me talk to Pete."

"What Pete?"

"Any Pete. Pete the bum, Pete the thief. You have a Pete, get him."

"No Pete."

"Then why'd you say 'What Pete?'"

"That 'Pete' and 'please' of yours and 'Fleet' and talking so fast. You got me confused."

"Hell I did. Then Turner then. Get me any Turner you have there and don't tell me you haven't one."

"We don't."

"Manure no Turner or Pete. You have a Stovin, right? Tell me you don't."

"We do. Two. Which one? Mister or the boy."

"Some boy, I'll bet, oh some boy. And he must be very proud of his pop too, or maybe the opposite's true. And you must be of both. Everyone must. Whole joint. Well get me either. No, just the elder. Tell him Shaney Fleet of Mitchell's Bar and Grill. He knows of me."

"Hold on." Comes back. "I'm afraid no one heard of you here or your grill. What do you want? You new? We didn't collect your trash yet today? If you're on the Northside, Mr. Fleet, it's because we had two unusual broken axles in our main trucks in one day, so we're far behind. Later we're making a double run."

"Listen, whoever you are. Who are you, just so I get a name?"

"Jennifer."

"Well you take steno, Jenny, right?"

"No, I only receive here and answer phones."

"But you can write, right? So if you please, get a pen and put this down to elder and boy and copies to Turner and Pete and whatever other upper-ups above your bosses if there are any. Ready?"

"No Turner and Pete. And I can't write fast. What I'll do is type, while you speak, though it's not my job, but okay: shoot, but short, as I got to also answer phones."

"Quote. Memo from S. Fleet to Stovin Private C.C. All you people will get back from him is trouble in the future if you continue hassling him which could mean broken windows in your garage, flat tires in your wheels, sand in your gas tanks and even a couple of cracks in your human heads. Because he's mad as all anything—that mad. One fire in his apartment's enough. One dead parrot in his ruins is too much. One almost burnt-down building he lived in and several almost lost burnt lives is all there's going to be. You getting this down, Jenny?"

"Most of it."

"I'll say this last part slowly. It's the most important. And whoever's listening on the extensions, steno this into your heads. Quote. Mr. Fleet likes his life all right but thinks it's worth cheap. And you know he's old enough not to go 'Oh help I'm sorry but I'm dying' or something or same time regret getting bopped around bad, but both for a good worthy fight if that's how it has to be. Though he's not such a dope to fight in a fight just to be in one, that you also have to see. So don't tempt him please. Lay off. Do and he'll about-face the police too. But that fire the other night is the next to last straw. He accepts that fire as the termination of the so-called garbage contract and nothing else, unquote, now you have that down or most?"

"The next straw. What was that?"

"Any way you want."

"I have it all then."

"Thank you. By the way, Jenny, if I can call you that, how can you work for such slobs?"

"You mean because we're in garbage? It doesn't come in here. We're enclosed and the trucks are washed and disinfected every day."

"I mean because they're crooks."

"They're not. Goodbye."

Police come an hour later. Different ones I've never seen before with a complaint against me from Stovin's. "They say you threatened personal and property injury to them. What's with you, Shaney? We hear nothing but great generous things from you at the precinct—from Brendon and Dom and Sergeant Lars. Stovin's even has it that you had their receptionist type what you said were whole quotes from you."

"Look at this." I show them the note. "Then they phoned and demanded a thousand. You know what it's about, right?"

"No."

I tell them.

"So what's it mean?" one of them says. "This your typewriter the note was written on and if so how come?"

"I could say no and you'd never know because that typewriter was in no better shape than my parrot and I'm sure they're both now junked."

"What parrot?"

I tell them. "But the typewriter's mine all right. I recognize the marks. The i without the dot and the half of e and f, not that I used it so much. It was willed to me by a dead customer."

"Hey Shaney, come here a sec," one of the regulars says.

"Not now, Lance."

"Not for a drink. What is it? You in a jam?"

"I said forget it, Lance, I'll handle it okay. A misunderstanding."

"You men are cops, am I right? I can tell by the way you're sturdily built and your strong walk and hair combed down across your foreheads so neat and you plainclothes all seem to favor the more stylish synthetic leather belted jackets these days. I know. I'm in men's clothes."

"You've something to tell us, sir?" one says.

"No. Only there's no misunderstanding between Shaney and me. He's a great gallant—he's the greatest finest most wonderfully thoughtful bartender there is—one from the old school, best they come. So anytime you need a backup for his good behavior or as a character witness, you see me."

"Lance," I say. "I said to stay out of it or get the hell out of here."

"Shaney, what is this, what I say? I never heard you talk to me like that in ten years, and just after I said that about you to them?"

"Excuse me, officers." I go over to Lance. "Look, I'm in trouble. Nothing I did but someone else to me. It's related to the fire so shut up, mind your business, and here's a free one even if you're half-loaded already and they could pull me in simply for giving you another drink, just so you know there's no animosity between us."

"Never, Shaney, never. I told you he was the best," raising his glass to them and sipping from it.

"I hate this trade," I say to the policemen, "or am beginning to. I think all my father's and grandfather's frustrations and long hours and tiredness from the bar business, not to say bad marriages because of it, are coming out through me from their graves. Stale piss in hell," and I pour myself a scotch. "I don't normally do this, honestly, never till closing at least," and I drink it down. "But today? Too many drunks. Too many Stovin's punks. Too much lousy of everything. The works, the works," and I pour another.

"So get out of it."

"Where? And why my crying on you? And who'll buy my bar with Stovin's demands hanging over me and business this slow?"

"If it's true, the business slow is one thing but don't tell the buyer you sell it to the garbage part."

"Can't do. No heart to. My father would turn over. My grandfather would smack me twice a night in my dreams for life. My greatgrandfather—he handhewn and shaped the oak

kegs that used to store the stuff—I never met him but I bet I'd
see him glaring at me in God's beard. I won't even mention my
lovely buried mother what she'd do. No. Once I get them off
my back somehow or they traipse away and business picks up,
though I don't see why for either, I'll sell, go around the world,
get a job tending bar or on a ship—no, not that anymore, I'd
get sick mixing drinks on the sea. Had it. I don't know what I'll
do. Drive a cab. By the way, you fellows like a nip?'' They
shake their heads. "Don't worry about Lance. That freebie
locked his teeth. And I know how superclean police are expected to be today, and I appreciate and respect that fact, but
you do work hard and dark hours and this is no bribe—you
heard Lance. I'm old-fashioned, just my way—a drink or sandwich on me and you're ready to go back on the street doing
double your duty, or even some pickled hardboiled eggs? I
make them like no one else. Maybe because nobody makes
them anymore.''

"Double vodka for both of us, but in coffee mugs and with a
little in it of that Mexican coffee liqueur to make it look and
smell like black coffee.''

I make their drinks under the bar. "I won't toast to you.''

"Good tact. Now, about this note. Why didn't you phone
us?''

"It's my typewriter. What could I have told you that you'd
believe? They got me going eighty different ways.''

"Then from when they phoned you today. Incidentally, too
many Mexican beans in mine. Just for the color and a little
smell it should go in, because now it's too sweet.''

I bring his mug back under the counter, take the coffee pot
off the heater and act as if I'm pouring more coffee in while with
my other hand I pour in more vodka from a bottle from the
speedrack by my knees.

"Mine's perfect as it is,'' the other policeman says.

"What do you know? I introduced you to these. But Shaney,
and thanks, just right now if you ever had to make it for me
again,'' and stirs the mug with the spoon I gave him, "when

they phoned you should've phoned us to be at the booth to get them if there was one."

"They would've seen me lift it. I only had ten minutes. They have to be watching me almost always to know so much of my movements, though I don't know from where. Maybe a window across the street. Or even that dog lady with the two giant wolves who just passed. But one hand on the receiver from me and I'm sure they wouldn't have been at the phonebooth and neither the envelope and tape underneath and then you really would've thought me nuts. Because you don't believe me much, do you?"

"Nice as you are, it's hard to. This nothing note. Your threatening calls. Phantoms on the street. From what window? Which dog lady?"

"You were staring straight out there same as me. You didn't see her?"

"No."

"And that street window across is for you to check. Rap on doors. Do what you're paid to. I'm only giving ideas. But you figure out how they know when I've no customers here and am phoning when I do and so forth. But you're not going to be any help."

"I'm not knocking it, and the lure would more than undo me, but maybe you tipple a little too much on the job when you shouldn't."

"Me? Only just recently. Ask anyone. Tell them, Lance. You ever see me throw one down before I closed?"

"I'm not sure what I should say for you after that last time, but no I never seen him drink since the mini one they almost had to force down his throat New Year's or was it Christmas eve?"

Police finish their drinks and get up to leave. "Anyway, you get something further on them, let us in on it quick. Otherwise, don't crankcall Stovin's anymore and subject yourself to arrest. They were being kind specifying us not to bring you in this time, not that you would've been held long, but next time on both you might."

"I get it. Thanks for coming."

I answer an apartment ad but then think I'm safer in the hotel. They want to burn me out again let them get past the desk and tobacco stand and all the traffic by the elevators and television lounge first. My room's small, bed too lumpy and soft, furniture's depressing, walls need mending, I miss my old things and parrot squawks and not having a refrigerator for early morning snacks and stove for breakfast and view of the planes and helicopters passing and sun rising and pigeons and sometimes gulls flying and tower tips of the lit bridge.

For a few days I get calls at four or five a.m. from Turner or Pete just saying before they hang up "Sleeping late?" or "Rise and shine!" and once reveille blown on what sounded like a potato flute accompanied in the end by a humming kazoo. After the third call I phone the police and say "All right, you want to see who's threatening who, start listening on my phone," but they say there's a state law forbidding them to tap hotels because they'd also be intercepting and snooping on other guests' calls.

So I tell the hotel not to put any calls through to me till eight a.m. But they still manage to get through with excuses to the nightclerk that my wife was just raped and is phoning me from a crisis center or some doctor from a hospital's calling saying he has to speak to me because my sister just had a stroke in her sleep.

"I have no sister, wife, child or anyone close enough like that to wake me before eight. Unless someone says my bar was broken into or is on fire, tell them to call back."

Next call to get through is from someone claiming to be a policeman who says my bar was just robbed. I say "I'll cab right over," hang up, call the precinct and find it's another lie. From then on I don't let any calls in of any kind till after I awake and phone downstairs and tell them it's okay.

Couple of weeks after I last see the police something's slipped through the door. I'm bent down behind the counter looking for a dropped bottle cap when I hear the mail slot flap clink. I run around the bar to the door. Envelope's on the floor. Same kind: my initials and address. I don't even pick it up but run outside and look around. Only a kid on a tricycle and a dog lady but a different one from two weeks before.

"Ned," I yell to the only customer in the bar, "don't let anyone touch the till."

"Sure, Shaney, but what about my potatoes and grilled cheese?"

I run after and catch up with the woman and her dog starts barking at me. "Pull it back, lady, call it off," and she says "Let go of me first." I didn't even know it but my hand's holding her shoulder. I let go and the dog stops barking but still snarls and I say "I'm sorry, but you just shove something through my door?"

"You kidding me?" and she walks away.

"If you're the one, lady, I got your face. I now know who you are, so don't try and come in my bar."

"And I got a pocketful of coins to phone the cops if you bother me again, crazy," and her dog starts barking less at me than at the air over his head.

I go back to the bar. Sandwich and potatoes are burning.

"Shaney, will you? Potatoes are okay welldone but you know I don't like my toast burned."

I run to the stove. "You should've gone around the bar and fixed it yourself."

"You might've thought I was stealing."

"Are you the one crazy now? Are you?"

"No, but I just thought—"

"Ahhh," and I flip the potatoes and sandwich over, toss the sandwich to the side because it's burned, prepare another one and smear butter on the grill and put the sandwich on it and open the envelope. Inside's a note typed on my old typewriter. It says: "Memory still serves? Well, set 2, same booth, mixed metaphors, clever clever, lost game, 12 mins this time as bank's a pinch packed, tho 2 thou now, sport, not won, your move, except 1st get on the ball and table your customer. Love."

"You see who put this through the mail slot, Ned?"

"No, I was staring into my glass. Still nothing in it but foam. Fill her up please?"

"Know what a mixed metaphor is?"

"Hey, if you're tossing away the burned sandwich, give it here for free but keep the new one cooking for me. I hate seeing good food go to waste no matter how bad it is. But mixed what?"

"Metaphor."

"Something to do with English in high school."

I give him the potatoes and burnt sandwich, flip over the other one and call George Ecomolos and ask him to drop by, it's very important, "Don't ask me why I didn't think of this sooner." He comes in that night and I say "I got a terrific problem," and tell him about it and he says "So what you want from me to do?"

"You know about it then?"

"Course I do, so?"

"So fight it, like me. Tell the police Stovin's is trying to run you around too. That way they won't think I'm insane and you can keep your business."

"On that I need a brandy. When'll you get the good import stuff from my country?"

"No call for it except you. Do what I ask though and I'll buy a case and give you it from me."

"Say, that a bribe now from you? I wouldn't've think that."

"No, just my gratitude."

"Go make it a dozen dozen cases but how I drink without a throat?"

"They wouldn't touch you."

"Stupo: they will."

"But you know people."

"They know bigger people. Bigger than bigger people. People bigger than biggest and more. Make mine look like scopic insects under glass to squash on thousand a time. Besides, I got fair deal you can say with Stovin's. Yes, but you have no tapedeck or fancy small recorder things under there or somewhere like in your shirt, do you, to catch my voice? Because you do and then don't tell me and erase all that went on before and now shut it off, you and me friends no more."

"Don't worry."

"Say, I worry. I don't then I'm one who insane."

"I've nothing to take down what you say except my head."

"Then clean erase that after we through too. No tell cops or anyone what I say about any things between me and them that I say now to you. Promise."

"Okay."

"Say 'I promise.' "

"Okay, I promise."

He puts out his hand and we shake.

"So this is the deal. It goes that I get all the storeowners who fight Stovin's about their garbage and win without my helping a finger to them, and they get to collect the rest."

"You'll end up with no one but me, if they even leave me a bar here for you to collect from."

"So I lose with one fight, but at least here I have slight chance of staying in business a lot more days. For you see, they could just have said 'Take a walk, baby, we run your garbage show now,' and me, no madman with my life, would have to have had obey. But my second cousin. I skip his name but he not someone that big in Stovin's or with their backers—of which group he belong he very sly about even to me. But he arrange as favor that they give me that other verbal deal out: to let me stay collecting garbage till they take away all my business in this neighborhood or almost, instead of just my closing my doors and going away when they say."

"So you'll be out entirely, because you once said you only collected around here."

"True. I do. It's a pact. Keep your trap shut, but we private carters carve the city into pieces. One gets West Side, other another side, and me I get here downtown. But Stovin's, they want my piece, they succeed without puffing and maybe later even get half this whole city, when before about twenty of us cut it up. But it's not so bad. I got savings stacked away and ideas for new businesses for me not concerned with any of them, or so far. And this is what happens a lot in garbage elsewhere. It happens too in lots other businesses here and there—chocolate bars, for one. You laugh, but check with candystores if not true. And news magazines distributing is another and some newspapers too, the weekly ones. And funeral parlors. That one and soon private carting my cousin say is the most. You think you want to open funeral parlor in city when and where you like just because you great undertaker and got degree from school to undertake? Laugh. All controlled. A few people, maybe same ones in garbage, say what you do or don't with funeral parlors and who even gets city licenses for them, and also orange juice. Everything liquid in citrus fruit.''

"Who is this Stovin?''

"The man?''

"So I know who I'm up against.''

"Exactly, not for sure, but hear big man with body too, plus tough son. So you're up against strong tall wall, two walls, no doors through them also, but don't you believe all that I hear: maybe they're both small and only their noise is like walls.''

"And the backers? I'm not naive, but what's it: an organized crime group of sorts?''

"Everything I hear is they're powerful people though maybe Stovin himself most powerful backer of them all and also this time in same business he back powerfully: garbage. He's not always in it: before he sold cigarettes to grocery stores. But I think I'm lucky they not kick or try to me out sooner, that's also the truth. They see this as upcoming neighborhood, more stores than before when For Rent signs were, so more garbage to pick up and what have you. So they move in, of course. Later I sell them my trucks, though not at the fairest price. But truth is, Shaney pal, you have to let them pick up your garbage sometime soon, for I be out by then and they won't let any new carter come around nor would any carter will.''

''One of the reasons I didn't—''

''Say, because of our old business together, years on years, I know,'' and he grabs and holds my hands. ''But told you—I be fine. Savings, wife who understands, and I tell you the truth now too, I'm sick of garbage after so long. She sick of it too, telling people what I do, even with all the money I once make, so stop concerning yourself for me and see them and agree to the first offer they say to take your garbage from now on.''

''All they want is two thousand and now probably more.''

''Pay it. Then they come around nice-like for your garbage, and that's the price you pay for not calling me before besides being so nice and for first saying to them no.''

''I don't have two thousand to spare.''

''Have it, find it, spare it, please.''

''That much? No way. They either have to collect my garbage for the fifteen to twenty-five extra dollars a month or run me out. I can't get a loan, not that I'd try, so I have no choice.''

''Then start running, I think, but I pray maybe you're right and you win after all.''

''Shaney,'' a customer says coming in, ''you won't believe it, I just got laid off, so you'll have to start me a new IOU tab with a double shot of rye.''

''Now I got to go,'' George says, ''and say goodbye last time in our lives for a while perhaps, for I don't want Stovin's people see me here and think I advising you to oppose. Thanks for the bad brandy,'' and he drinks up, kisses my hands, pats my customer's back and goes.

I phone Stovin's and say ''Jenny, don't hang up, this is Shaney Fleet again. I'm sorry for the unease I might've caused you the other day with my being rude, but could you please tell your boss or Turner or Pete if they're there—''

''I already told you.''

''Then just Mr. Stovin or son or the accountant who might know of me or any salesman that I'm ready to give in, this isn't a trick, and I'd like your company to start carting for me.''

"For whatever it's worth, Mr. Fleet, I'll pass it on."

"You're a doll."

Next day while I'm tapping a keg in the basement cooler right under the bar a customer shouts out "Shaney, a paper just flew through the mail chute—want me to pick it up?"

I run for the stairs, then down the two steps I got up, as the rod in the keg could explode the way I left it halfway in and the beer ready to spout, and finish tapping it and run upstairs and around the bar to the outside. Policeman on the beat, police car cruising the street, a group of kids tossing around iceballs and making noise as they walk home from the nearby parochial school, overhead pretty close a seaplane, faraway the barking at the same time of fierce dogs, around me snowflakes. I pick up the envelope and read the note inside. "Our answer," it says in letters painstakingly penciled and filled in from an alphabet stencil, "is same place last chance $2500 now go to bank dont for a moment phone or delay."

I take one of my pickled eggs, mix lots of garlic cloves from the jar with it, chop them up and under the counter stick them in the note envelope and spit a goodsized wad into it and tell the two customers "I'll be right back, get another beer free if you want but don't let a soul in even if they knock." I stick a little billy in my back pocket just in case and go outside, lock the door and go to the bank and write on the back of a withdrawal slip "2500 death germs I hope you get from my spit, you bastards, and may the garlic not be enough to ward them off, don't ask me what good or symbol to you is my putrid egg," and put that in the envelope on top of about twenty blank withdrawal slips and seal it up, get on line and when it's my turn I go to the teller and put the envelope on the counter between us and just as he grabs and brings it down to him I say "Excuse me, I forgot something, just a second," and rifle through my coat pockets. "Damn, I must've left it in the bar—can I have that back?" He gives me the envelope and I leave the bank and go to the phonebooth on Second and Prescott another block away and wait for a young woman in the booth to finish arguing with her father about how it's none of his damn business where she was last night and earlier today—"Do I ever ask you where you are or what you do? No, so shut up or I won't come home," and slams down the receiver and scoops up her change. I look at her, maybe coldly because I'm suddenly sorry for her dad, and she stares at me as she leaves the booth and says "What do you want?" and I shake my head and step out of her way and go inside, turn around, see that she's gone and nobody else seems to be looking at me, feel under the shelf, find the tape which is so sticky that my fingers have difficulty getting off it, and fasten the envelope to it and leave the booth and go around the corner and head back to the bar. But I stop, a block away, say "Hell, came this far, let me see who they are," and hail a cab and have him drive me to the opposite side of the busy oneway avenue about thirty feet up from the booth, and doublepark.

Couple of seconds later a man goes into the booth, seems to jiggle the coin return button same time he sticks a finger in the return slot and pockets what he gets and moves on.

"Cabs don't make money standing," the driver says.

"Don't worry, I'll make it pay."

"How?"

"A good tip."

"How much?"

"Listen, standing is also part of the cab-driving job and I said I'll make it pay."

"But how much?"

"Five bucks. Nothing happens a few minutes more, I'll walk."

Three minutes later, meter still running, cabby never stopping his grumbling, my stomach nervous from the excitement of what I've done with that envelope on the tape and this wait and what I might find and head clotted not with the idea of stomping the guy or guys but to grab whoever they are just to see who so I know them if I already don't and maybe to ask lots of whys, a man goes into the booth, gets the envelope, opens it and looks inside, drops it to the floor and leaves. Few feet away he snaps his fingers, goes back, picks up the envelope, opens it almost prissily this time, takes out a withdrawal slip by one of its corner tips, rubs it on the sidewalk back and forth and puts it in his wallet and throws the envelope into a trash can near the booth but misses and it lands on the street and the slips fall out and are picked up by the wind and sail in circles around the can and a couple up in the air and away.

"He's who you're waiting for?" the cabby says.

"Yes."

"There's to be trouble between you of any kind, pay up and get out now. I don't want to spend the rest of my day filling out police forms on what might turn out to be a lucrative snowstorm for my cab."

I give him fifteen dollars and tell him to keep it all if he just drops me a little ways behind the man on the man's side of the street and that there'll even be more if the man jumps in a car and we have to follow him by cab. Meter reads $2.85 and he puts the flag up and says "Cop comes, tell him you were just stepping out and then leave." We cross the avenue and follow the man for a minute. He walks fast, wiping his hands with a handkerchief, and when I decide no one's with him and he's not going to a car I say "Now," and the cabby says "Now what?" and I say "Where'd you go to school? Stop right here!" and he does and I get out and walk after the man. The man hears the cab accelerate and stares after it as it passes and twists around and sees me and walks faster. I recognize him I think but don't know for sure. I walk faster after him thinking where have I seen him if I have? In the bar? Somewhere on the street near it or maybe in my hotel or my old neighborhood or the diner I go to every morning now for muffins and coffee? He starts running and I run after him. Zigzags between some cars when the redlight's against him and I have to do that too, and it's snowing harder and I could easily lose him in the falling snow. I'm lean and he's pretty heavy though we're both about the same age it seems but his coat's long and bulky while mine's short and light. He also has tall heels on his boots and I have my special bartender shoes with the rubber ripple soles that almost throw me forward. He runs into a lady when I've just about caught up with him and her umbrella flies, paper bag she was carrying goes elsewhere and a few rolls roll out, woman landing in two men's arms just before she would have hit the ground faceways. The man spins around from the crash, arms windmilling to stop him from slipping, sees me right next to him and throws his hands up in front of his face, but I'm so mad at who I see he is that I come down on his head with my fist and then the other fist to his ear while he can't keep his feet from sliding from under him and he falls down and when he's on his back on the ground but his head rising I get my knee on him and slap him twice in the cheeks and then take him by his coat shoulders and slam his head on the pavement a couple of times though I only meant to shake him in the air.

His lids close, body goes limp. I say "Get up, you mother," but he doesn't move. "Come on, don't bluff me, I'm not going to hit you anymore, so get up."

An old man's screaming, back and hands pressed against a building wall, then walks off. Woman's cursing while she picks up her rolls, blows the snow off them and puts them in her pocketbook. I raise one of the man's lids and only see what looks like a dead eyeball. I put my hand under his coat; he's beating. The two men who caught the woman stand over me and look like they want to grab and throw me to the ground but by their weak faces I know won't and I say "Don't, listen, this man, he set fire to my apartment three weeks ago or else helped because he left a note saying something of mine was going up, and it was for nothing I did. Nothing. I own a bar. Mitchell's Grill four blocks back. They're hoods he belongs to and trying to ruin me."

"We don't know about hitting a man like that though," one of the two men says.

"But I lost everything in that fire. You name it. My parrot who I loved and lost her with all my personal belongings too. Someone call the police while I keep guard over this guy."

"All right," the man says. "Someone should probably phone them."

"You do it. From that booth over there."

"I'm not getting in like that, since how do I know you're the truth?"

"It's the truth, the truth."

"That's what you say, though the man you dumped might be in the right."

"Would I ask you to get the police for me if he was?"

"You might be just saying that to later get up and run away once one of us goes to call. At least with two of us here you might not try."

"You," I say to the other man. "Don't listen to him. Please call."

"What this gentleman says about your maybe being wrong could be right. I'm staying. Send someone else."

"Someone, please, call the police," I say to the small crowd, snow falling on us, starting to stick. "This man's a crook, was trying to extort money from me or was definitely in on it some way. I'm the owner of Mitchell's Bar and Grill—Shaney Fleet, the police in this precinct know me—the Fifteenth. Ask them, phone them now."

The woman the man crashed into is gone. Her umbrella flew into the street and a bus smashed into it and now cars are running over it. Other people left the crowd when I spoke and a few new ones joined, asking everyone else but me what I was speaking about and why's the man on the ground and was that screaming before coming from here, though no one offers to call the police nor gives any sign he's going to.

"Then let's carry him to the phonebooth so I can call the police," I say to the two men. "That way you can stay with us and he's getting pneumonia down there."

"And if his skull or arm's broken or spine and he gets five times worse because we carried him and maybe dies, he'll sue for hospital bills and damages or his survivors will and who'll lose? You and we will if you have anything to, I know I do, so let's leave him here."

I lift the man off the ground.

"I said to leave him!"

"And I say to get the hell out of my way if you're not going to help," and get the man in a fireman's carry and carry him to the booth a half-block away. The two men walk alongside and several other people follow us. The man's still unconscious it seems. His arms hang. He's breathing. Blood's running out of his head down my front. I kick away some snow, set him down, sit him up, pull him inside the booth till his back's braced against a wall, button him up to his neck, lay my coat over his legs and boots, with my handkerchief dab the gash in his head and wipe the snow off his nose and hair, as his hat seems to have gotten lost somewhere from the time I first saw and then caught him. I pat his pockets and thighs and chest thinking maybe he has a gun. There is none but is a folded-up switchblade. I put it in my pocket.

"What'd you just take there?" one of the two men says.

"A knife." I show it. "Think I want to get stabbed by him? Here, if you think I'm a thief," and I throw it into the street. "That better?"

"What, for some kid on junk to find and stick in one of us?" He gets the knife and holds it.

I dial the police. The officer says "Does he need an ambulance?" and I say "He just seems knocked out like any number of drunks at my bar and his bleeding's about stopped, but I haven't that much sympathy for him so do what you want," and she says "A car and an ambulance if the hospital has one right away will be right there."

I hang up and say to the two men "To explain things, so you won't go crazy attacking me thinking I want to steal, what I'm going to do now is try and find evidence on this man to see if he's linked to the people who set fire to my apartment and are trying to kill my business place," and the more talking one says "Why can't you wait that for the cops?"

"Because they and the hospitals have a reputation of losing

evidence out of bungling, I read, or when they just don't want something to get known, and I know damn well they also won't tell me what they find if I ask. Understand I'm not saying the police are in on it against me intentionally or in any way. But you can't believe what I've gone through with them so far with my bar, so for all sorts of reasons like my health I have to start relying on myself, all right?'' and the man says "Okay, go ahead, but everything you do and say we're telling the cops, if we can remember it,'' and a young man behind them says "I'll jot it down,'' and takes out a pen and pad and writes.

I search the man's coat and pants pockets. Wallet he has I open but it has nothing but money and my note and a photo of an old man and woman in it and I put it back in his pants. Tissuepack, paperback, keys attached to a nailclipper and religious medal and that's all. The man's eyes open a few times and I say "How are you? You'll be all right,'' and he says "What're you doing, get out of my stuff,'' and shuts his eyes. I feel for his pulse but don't get any mostly because I don't know how to get a pulse if it's not just squeezing the wrist for a beat. Then the police car comes and when they take a look at the man, one says "You should've thought of this when you called us—he seems like he's dying and needs an ambulance,'' and I say "One's supposed to be on the way,'' and he says "Where is it then?'' and puts in a call for one.

The police search me, find the billy, tell the two men and the young one with the pad and pen to stay. They wrap a blanket around the man I hit, massage his hands and keep the crowd back and a couple of people from trying to make phonecalls from the booth when they didn't see the man on the floor, and soon at the same time two ambulances come from opposite ends of the avenue and the drivers argue for a while over who's entitled to take the man while the two doctors from the different hospitals work on him. Finally one policeman says to a driver "You, for no good reason, just you,'' and that ambulance team puts the man on a stretcher and takes him away.

More police come and they divide me and the three men into

two groups and while they're asking me questions I overhear the more talkative of the two older men say "All I know is I saw that guy hit him, the barowner he says he is, few times real hard in the face and I think once with that club you took off him, but on that I'm not so sure. I didn't see him provoked—he just went wild, ran after him shouting, knocked over a lady and attacked."

I say to the policeman interviewing me "What that fellow just said's not true," and I show them the note I got and say "The one I sent the man through the phonebooth shelf is in his wallet, but that's gone with him and probably lost by now," and the talkative man yells "Yeah, but you opened his wallet before because you said you didn't trust the police force, so how does anyone know what notes you might've stuck in there?"

"Did you see me?"

"I didn't see you not do it."

"And your friend?"

"He's not my friend. I don't know him and he's got a mouth for himself."

"I didn't see you take or insert in the wallet anything like paper," the other man says. "But my vision isn't the sharpest except for bigger things, such as your beating up for no justification it seems the man they took away."

"What are you guys? You with the man I hit? You were there from the start, so maybe you are."

"Excuse me," the young man says to the police. "But I have it in my notes where, and I quote, 'suspect removes unconscious man's wallet—seemingly unconscious—peers inside, puts it back in man's same pants pocket left side,' but there's nothing about removing anything from the wallet."

"Did you *see* him taking anything out though?" a policeman says. "Or putting anything in?"

"I'm not sure. I was doing a little looking but mostly writing."

"Let's see that." The young man tears some sheets out of the pad and the policeman reads from them. "'Victim, up till now

42

seemingly unconscious against glass panel of booth, says "Stop searching me" to assailant but assailant does not.'"

"I was looking for the exact names and maybe his contacts of the people who've been hounding me, but maybe this pen-and-pad kid's in with them too. Before I thought they were all just passerbys—passersby—whatever the hell they are, it is, walking past. But now, well—"

"That's all I am," the young man says. "I live with my mom and aunts. I'm a journalism major on my way home from school uptown and if it's all right now I'd like to leave to study and eat."

A policeman says "We got their names and pad notes and it's a shitty day besides, so why don't we let the witnesses go?" and the other policemen agree and the three men leave.

I give the police the names of several detectives at their precinct and say "Ask them about me and the man I hit who I described to them earlier from my fire. Also why not check those two men and even the kid and see if they work for Stovin's Carting Company or just who they do work for and if it's in any way connected to garbage collection or goon-type crime and if the kid really is a student and what school. He didn't seem like a liar, but how do we know?"

"This isn't a police state," a policeman says. "And if this incident ever goes to trial, your lawyer can handle all the who-works-for-who and so forth."

"It's going to trial all right, but by me dragging into court that phony the ambulance took away."

"Good. But now I'm sorry but we got to bring you in for assault and intent with a dangerous weapon," and I say "My billy? Come on, your microscope guys will find it stayed in my pocket as protection with no blood or head marks on it except for maybe some drunk's arm a year back if any blood got on it then and can last that long. But I want to tell you something before you take me in."

"If he dies you'll feel horrible—get in."

I get in back of the car and say to him in front "It's true. I never killed anybody, even when I could've when I was in the service, but wouldn't even do it overseas. Few times I fought I shot over the enemy's heads.''

"So they could live to kill your buddies. Oh, guys like you I don't understand and would've shot in the back in the army if I knew what you were doing. But that man you punched you might've been mistaken, you know. He could've just opened your envelope because he was making a call and his fingers out of nothing to do wandered under the shelf and fiddled around with the envelope you say was there but which we never found a speck of except for the tape you could've put there yourself, till he caught on what it might be.''

"Then why'd he put my note from it into his wallet?''

"We don't know he did yet. But if he did, then maybe as a joke.''

"I don't get it. To give to someone else?''

"That too. Maybe he wanted to play it on someone else. But what I was suggesting was maybe he kept the note to show someone how much a joke had been played on him in the booth.''

"With my spit all over it he'd put it in his wallet?''

"The spit would've been dried by then.''

"But he rubbed it off on the sidewalk.''

"That's what you claim.''

"Back and forth he rubbed, back and forth.''

"Someone else but you saw? Not those three duds.''

"Then how do you also explain I recognized him as the note-leaving guy at my bar from the fire?''

"Your word against his again.''

"Hell with it. Long as I know he's involved, that's enough for me.''

"Good for you," and he calls in that we're coming, other man gets out to wipe the snow off the windshield and we drive to the stationhouse.

I'm booked, they ask if I have a lawyer. I say "I never had much use for anyone who takes so much money for what with a little hard brainwork I can do myself, not that I ever even much trusted them either," and they say they'll have one appointed to me then as that's the law.

"The law," I say, "the law. Well just see if I don't refuse your appointee," and ask and they say okay for me to call my bar. I get Hector, one of the two men I asked to stay and say "Anyone there but you?"

"Boo, but you told us not to."

"I know, but anyone else try and come in or call?"

"No and it's getting late and we got to be moving. Even for money it's not worth staying here anymore—my wife will kill me."

"One last favor. I'm in the police station for something I did and am giving my keys to the police to close my place. Stay there till they come. Don't let anyone but them in and ask for their badges."

"I don't ask cops for badges. Question them and you anger and get trouble from them. They got uniforms on, they're cops. You, I don't ask what happened less you tell."

"Thanks, but listen. Take all the money out of the cash register and from the cigar box below and tip glass next to the juicer and put it all in one of the brown paper bags there by the coffeemaker."

"Wait a minute. Where's the coffeemaker?"

"By the juicer. Double the bags, in fact, as the change will weigh a ton. Leave the nickels if you want and keep the rest on you alone, Hector, not Boo. He's okay, I'm not saying he's not and I know he's your friend. But he's a little dim, right? and wait till I call you again at home. What's your number?"

"I don't even see where's the juicer and I'm looking."

"Right by the register. But your phone number."

He gives it.

"Listen, Hector, I'm putting my faith in you two but you especially. And I'm not saying you're dishonest by any means, because would I be asking you to do this for me if I was? But I know how much money there is between the register and cigar box. Tip glass probably another few bucks."

"How much you think altogether?"

"Why you asking? Besides, you'll have plenty of time to count it at home. But there's twenty in it for you and Boo, ten apiece and okay, for you another five, just for doing this for me."

"What're you afraid of, cops on the take?"

"A little, yes. They've done it with other barowners. They slip in the place because of some minor infraction nobody's followed for fifty years or an anonymous phone complaint maybe made by them in a disguised voice, and while one's questioning the bartender, boom, half the register money's suddenly gone. Where'd it go? 'Oh, I don't know,' they say, 'you accusing us?' getting tough. 'You yelling corrupt?' Ah. Maybe, probably the ones who come to close will be clean and great but I can't take chances, though forget the bottles they might cart away before they return my keys, and the steaks."

"How am I to tell Boo you only want me to hold the money? He's big and already a bit tanked and mean from all the booze he drank."

"I told you guys only free beer."

"Not me, him, but you also told us you'd be right back."

"Okay, wait, let me think. After the police come take the money straight to Kelly's Bar instead and give it to Kelly to hold."

"What're you now, all of a sudden don't trust me?"

"I trust you but Kelly's always been all right with me and he knows where to hide money, you might not."

"I got a floorboard in my place for stashing away stuff. And now I told you that you know something about me that nobody else does."

"I'd still rather have Kelly."

"You know, being so all right with people isn't what I learned about him. Why I don't go in there and others is he gives change for five dollars too many times when you give him a ten. And how you know he'll be there?"

"Call him. If he's not, call me at the 15th Precinct right back. But just take the money if he is which he will be, he's like me, he never leaves and he'll be honest with me or else he knows he won't get favors back. I'll try and call you later tonight or the morning and you'll have put down by then how much you gave Kelly, okay?"

"Okay, but I still don't like that you don't trust me or what Boo might do."

"I do trust you, I do, and when I get back you have a home at the bar for free food and booze for a couple of days, Boo too. Now put him on."

"Yeh," Boo says.

"Boo, this is Shaney."

"Yeh, I know, Hector said, so?"

"So Boo, I don't care, I'm not normally like this as you know and don't give me that tough 'so' stuff too, but big as you are and sober and mean as you might be that day, if you give Hector any flack about the job I just gave him to do I'll beat your ass black and blue with my billy, I swear, and much worse than that I'll ban you forever from my bar, you got?"

"Yeh. I'll keep myself straight."

"Good man and thanks."

I give the police my bar keys and two of them leave to lock up. I ask the sergeant if he could put a guard on the bar tonight for I'm almost sure Stovin's men will try and firebomb the place or smash in all the plate glass. He says "We're shorthanded as it is. And I can't see why your bar rates a special guard when you're the person being held and charged for maybe clobbering to death one of the group you accuse of harassing you."

"You'll put that down in writing for my bar's insurance company?"

"I'll put your face down in writing if you don't smarten up."

"And threaten me again and I'll have whoever it is supposed to know about police threats know about you."

"Quick, someone—Angelo, get over here," he yells to a

policeman, "and get this asshole out of my sight before I lose my cool altogether and level him and then you guys will lose your protective sergeant for another few weeks."

Angelo sits me down, gets me coffee and tells me to lay off the sergeant. "He's been called down before for busting a suspect's jaw and we can't afford to have him kicked off the force." Later he checks with the sergeant and tells me that the court which will talk about bail and my appointed lawyer for my assault and possible manslaughter case doesn't open till tomorrow at ten and I'll have to spend the night in a detaining cell upstairs.

I'm given a blanket, towel and toothbrush and taken to the cell. Three other men share it. I want to call Hector but the guard tells me "As a first-nighter you already made your limitation of one call." I eat and while the guards and other prisoners watch TV in the common room shared by an entire floor of cells, I lie on my upper-bunk cot and think and think about my situation and end up thinking there's nothing to think about how to end the situation and there's no way I can stop and my only hope's that Stovin's will think or say they've had enough of me and our situation and let it drop.

Cells are locked up right after the late evening news, we're given a doughnut and apple juice snack, our light's turned off though there's still the glow from the common room lamps and TV the guards continue to watch, the men in the cell talk in the dark about the movie they'd just seen.

"I liked it because it was real."

"Real how? When you shoot someone there's supposed to be holes and blood."

"Maybe there was but on the small screen compared to a theater's you couldn't see them and also the color was bad."

"What makes you say the movie wasn't especially made for TV?"

"Excuse me, fellas," I say.

"Because I saw it in its uncut version a year ago."

"I don't believe you."

"And I don't believe you don't believe me."

48

"Listen, you weasel."

"Excuse me. I don't mean to cut into your conversation, so anyone wants to tell me to shut up, go ahead. But as long as I'm here, and you want to know anything more about me I'm a barowner of a cheap place called Mitchell's on East 5th Street, but any of you know anything about a garbage company called Stovin's on D and Sand?"

"No."

"No."

"No, why?" the man below me says.

"You know them?"

"No, what I got with garbage? I'm curious and just talking like the other two—what else we to do?"

I make it brief about what's happened to me the last few weeks and ask if they've heard of anything like that happening downtown and they all say no and then just generally in town and they say no and then what any of them would do if he was me.

"Seems like two dudes just hustling you and your apartment fire wasn't connected or they overfanned it to a mistake," one of the men across from me says. "Don't bother them again and they'll go away."

"Never give someone advice that could cost him his life," the man above him says.

"Why, he'll come back to haunt me?"

"His brothers might, weasel."

"What I'd do," the man below me says, "is lease for a cheap fee your bar for a year and take a southern vacation but tell your friends you went north, because you'll get yourself killed resisting back to them like that."

"But you never heard of them or the two men, Turner or Pete? Just by your voice you sounded like you might. And it's all right if you did, as I won't mention where I met you or your name. I just want to know what they think they have to do to me before they stop."

"I said no, go to sleep."

"Goodnight," the other two say.

"Night, fellas." I fall asleep and am dreaming of getting into our old car in the neighborhood I lived in with my folks years ago. They're what they look like and in the same clothes as in my photos I lost of them in the fire and I'm the same size, age and face I'm now but act much younger, so I guess I'm supposed to be in this dream about eleven or twelve which is when we had that car, when all four doors slam closed and my head flashes white, car my father puts the ignition key in explodes, dream suddenly ends and I feel tremendous pain in my brains and hands and legs, white breaks apart into stars and dashes and dots like a universe starting up and then I have to puke, I'm screaming and awake and want to bawl like a kid the pain in my head's so great, but I just go out and next when I'm awake the cell's lit and someone's sticking needles in my arm and another's sucking out something from my mouth and nose with a hose and next when I'm awake I'm on a stretcher zipping through an empty hall except for some police and a couple of rough-looking men in cuffs and I first think it's another dream because my head and sight's so indistinct and then I see and think it clear. I'm wet with sweat all over it feels, pissed or shit in my pants because something like that stinks and seems to be me and my lips are sticky and I got blood on my stretcher and chest.

"No problem, you'll be okay," someone says, man walking next to me it is with his clipboard clapping the wall and I say yes.

"You can hear?"

"Hear, yes."

"Guy's got great recovery," the bearer in front of us says and I say yes. "Good pair of ears too."

I reach up to feel where it is that still hurts so much in the head but the man next to me says "Put it down, don't touch, I'm warning you, Fleet. That's a clean dressing the doc put on and I'm responsible, so I'll slap your hand right off your wrist."

I drop my hand if I ever got it up and again go out.

"You can't have me anymore, Mr. Fleet," a woman says.
"Wha?"

"I said I'm afraid you can't have me anymore. Want me to speak louder? You see, to put it in plain layman's language, the criminal court, in the person of the judge of such, appointed me as your lawyer because of your own inexplicit and, to me personally, rather witless self-destructive reasons why you didn't need one, but now I have to unappoint myself because there's no longer a criminal case. We just received corroboration from the D.A. that the man you beat up dropped charges against you.—Forgive me, but we were talking about this before, don't you remember?"

"Huh?"

"You certain you're even conscious now?"

"Let me see."

Eyes open all the way. Light from the outside's in the room. Cages on the windows padlocked. Smell of public school cafeteria food. I'm asleep under white sheets in a men's ward or was. Now I'm up. My mind sort of, not my neck or back. And it's snowing again or never stopped. And birds, I hear birds, but it's this whistler in the next bed like a whole flock of them and most of the pain's gone in my head.

"I don't want to disturb you if you still want to doze."

"No, I want to stay up. Why my here?"

"I already told you."

"Why my here?"

"Well, your face is more alert. Has to be a good sign, particularly with all the painkiller they put in. You're healthy and perky again or thereabouts—congrats. I'm Janie Pershcolt, remember? We just had a long involved conversation about your life and bad breaks of late, but all the time you weren't even awake? How can that be? Anyway, I'm your court-appointed etcetera, not that I'm available to you now, etcetera—and you won't flake out on me again?"

"Try not to."

"Hungry? Want food, Mr. Fleet? Mr. Fleet, are you there?

Food. Pudding. Potatoes, munch munch, and buttered bread. You should be starved after two days of just tubes. They're giving out the trays now and before you said you didn't."

"Still don't. Stomach."

"You're not nauseous. If you are, be a friend as I've been to you and forewarn so I can step aside? Anyway, as I told you previously, the reason you're here is you were hit on the head with a pipe two nights ago or with some comparably solid instrument and possibly thrown off your bed, remember that?"

"Not talking about or happening it."

"Why would, assuming he did, and looks like to me, one of your fellow cellmates do that or any combination of the three? In your sleep conversation you said you only dreamed getting bonked."

"Looks like to me? Combination three?"

"Forgive me, but are you accusing all three prisoners of participating in the attack?"

"The guard?"

"The guard too or alone? Which, if either, and what's your basis for stating that?"

"Let me think."

"That's a pretty wild charge, Mr. Fleet. Earthshaking anytime the lawbreaker's the law. I'm not a prosecuting attorney or your lawyer anymore, but because my field is criminal jurisprudence and the penal system and so forth, I would like to know."

"Let me think."

"I hope there's no permanent brain damage. I mean I know there's none permanent or otherwise because the doctor told me there's not, so don't let me worry you, but I hope there isn't."

"I don't feel it. Please, Ginny, let me think."

"Janie, Janie. —So how are you today?" she says to the next bed.

"Fine and dandy, ma'am, and you?"

"I'm hardly the one in the hospital plus incarcerated, but I feel terrific today. I adore snow." And suddenly to me "Quick, Shaney, what's your name?"

"My what?"

"Name, quick, your name."

"Shaney Elborn Fleet."

"Quick, what do you do and where and all that?"

"Own a bar. Barowner. Ten to one. Tend one too. I do. One twenty-three East 5th Street, postal code forgot. Mitchell's Bar and G. B and Grill. Bar and Grest, Rest, please—these questions hurt my head. And will you please stop whistling?" I say to the next bed. "It's a nice tune and you whistle well but it's killing me."

"Ever you say, pal."

"No, you're all right," she says. "Quick response, natural verbal confusion, though what you said made sense. But your three ex-cellmates say they didn't touch you. That while they slept you must have rolled off your bunk to the floor because you weren't familiar with upstairs sleeping, and no one could find the pipe or comparable solid instrument."

"Forget what I said of the guard. I just wanted to know if he knew anything. But the police won't prosecute?"

"You have some proof?"

"My head. What the doctors said. For why they think a pipe?"

"Type of skull gash. No fist did it. Broke the skin and a bit of bone and was caused not by your head hitting something but something hitting it. Sixteen stitches. That's what your turban's all about. Concussion they'll only know when—"

"Because they're after me those bastards and word in, they did, got the, to the jail to nail me, get me, that's it, has to be, that sonofabitch whoever did it, so what the hell else is new? Don't you see, and excuse me for my cursing and muddledness, but they're all from the same group."

"Who? You claiming the pipe, apartment fire and reason for your delivering that street beating are all related to the garbage can company you complained about in the police report I read?

You have to have something backing you better than wild charges or that company will nail you for defamation of everything and then you'll really go to jail and pay. Because as I said before. Well, I don't know if I said it but I'll say it now. I'm not saying you're a fabricator, Mr. Fleet. Or that anything you said happened to you couldn't have in this city individually or even as you stated be intertwined. But so far you've no case. One, there's no bludgeoning weapon, so maybe the forensic medic was mistaken and your head did roll off your bed and hit a shoe we'll say or your own elbow on the floor and made that gash like a pipe might make. Two, three men in your cell are prepared to swear that none of them brained you or at least neither of them witnessed it. And three, it's not as if you're a prison guard who got piped, so who's really that concerned? Be realistic. To most people, judges or otherwise, what occurs in a prison cell is your own fault for getting in there, even if how you got in turns out to be an error of the police or court. And four, that man on the street you beat up says he won't reveal his name and address for fear his wife will find out he was in town with his mistress that day when he told her he was to be a hundred miles from here on business. That's why he won't press charges against you, which when you think of it could make sense. And five, if that fire was deliberately started, then it was an arsonist's dream job. Forgive me for butting in more than I was appointed to. But if you—pipe story aside, which might have been a personal affair between you and one or all of your ex-cellmates and so not something they want to disclose—have any doubt you're telling the truth about this Stovin's group or anyone you've accused so far, then for your own sake, and I say this with all my professional expertise and individual sincerity, don't you think it'd be wise to maybe see a psychiatrist?''

"Thanks very much, but didn't the police look in the man's wallet for my note?''

"Note? Hold it. Maybe I'm the one losing my memory now.''

"The note, my note. Under the phone shelf. I told the police he—''

"Oh yeah. Now how could they? He wasn't the one brought in and arraigned."

"But they looked for his name and address, didn't they? Since my note was the only thing in his wallet besides money, because I looked in it myself, they had to have seen it."

"Even if you didn't put the note in and they did find it, which I'm only being hypothetical for argument's sake about, it would most likely be classified as illegal evidence because the note wasn't what they would have been legally searching for."

"If they found a loaded gun in his wallet while they were only searching for his address, would that be illegal evidence too?"

"Then they might have questioned him, though maybe only to find out how he was able to fit a gun in his wallet—do you get what I mean?"

"Excuse me, but can I check out of here when I want?"

"According to the call before, they're not holding you for anything anymore and you don't seem to have a serious concussion the way you're now making noise, so I think so—of course. But why leave when you can stay a few more days courtesy of the city before they transfer you to a paying hospital, especially with the state of your head. I didn't mention that they said you'll have a permanent deep dent there around the metal plate, which is just how bad the blow was."

"Because I won't feel safe anyplace but in my bar or hotel room. There I got my own locks and regular grounds and my own form of weapons if I want. Here, who knows what can happen. Another pipe at night. Dent in a dent perhaps where I'll end up with a tin helmet for a head, or maybe something in my food. Sure, by your look I can tell I must sound to you like I feel way overpersecuted. And whatever I say after it to explain why I've these fears will make me sound even more so till they think I'm too crazy to go home, so why even stay here and risk being tossed in a mental ward?"

"If you insist, nobody can stop you, not that I like you roaming around outside with your head in such physical shape. Though if you do leave and need a lawyer for future advice on these matters I'm not saying you don't legitimately fear, I do have a private practice too. This should be confidential between us if you don't mind. I'm not by city law allowed to take for money one of the defendants I was initially appointed by the court to defend for free, even after the charges against him are dropped, and my fees compared to lawyers of much less caliber and human sympathy are relatively cheap. Here's my card." She takes one from her briefcase and puts it in my hand. "Maybe you'll forget it's there, though your attention span seems to be progressing by the second," and she opens a sidetable drawer. The whistler says "Hey, lady, what are you doing in my things?" and she says "Sorry," goes around my bed and opens what I suppose is my drawer, takes out my wallet, says "Mind?" and sticks the card in. "One positive thing I can probably do for you now is get your nurse," and she touches my finger and goes.

"Wait!"

"What?"

"Advice. What do I legally do if Stovin's group comes at me again?"

"Why should they? If what you say is true, then they gave you your lumps. If what you say isn't, then what's to worry about?" and she goes.

Nurse comes in with two policemen and says "Actually our policy is if you can stand by yourself once we get you out of bed, you can walk out of here if you have your court release, so let's first see if we can make you stand."

They help me out of bed. She says "Ready?" and I nod and they let go of me and I keep standing though sag at the knees somewhat and really have to fall.

"Good boy. They'll get you dressed. Truth is it's only because there was a big knifefight in your jail last night that I'm kind of hurrying you, Mr. Fleet, as they're now recovering in the halls. Besides of course we always no matter how many fights and suicides a night in there need all the beds we can get for the injured prisoners coming from the outside. Stay out of trouble and best of luck."

I'm discharged, go to my hotel, am given a new room, with a view, as they thought I ran out on the bill and wouldn't be back, rest and that night call Hector at home. His wife, when I tell her my name, says "He out, be back." She says that every hour for three hours till I call and say in a phony accent and voice with a tissue over the mouthpiece "Hey, dis is Jake," who's a drinking pal of his, "de old crow in?" an expression for Hector I've heard Jake use.

Hector gets on and says "Jake, you dumb jerk, how do they say it: so what's it by you?"

"Hector, how come you don't want to speak to me?"

"Shaney? Not speak to you how? What's with this Jake? Anything happen to him?"

"Your wife told me you weren't in."

"I just came through the door while she was talking. How are you? Heard you were really hurt bad."

"Heard from who?"

"Why the exam? I don't know: cops. One on the street. Not on the street where he told me but one from the street I remembered when I spoke to him by phone at the police station as to if anything happened to you and he said you'd been busted over the head real bad. I'm really sorry for you. How do you feel?"

"What's this policeman's name?"

"I don't know his name. His voice, on the phone, and don't ask what kind of voice. Just a voice, a rough one on and off the phone that I remembered by ear. Maybe I only think it's him I spoke to."

"Hector, how come I'm not believing you? It's funny but now that both my ears are bandaged over and I've got to strain to hear anything, I'm starting to hear better than I ever did before."

"I don't understand. Speak clearer. What's all that jumble about?"

"Speak clearer. Jumble. You don't understand me. Bull. I don't like this, that's what I'm saying. That you didn't want to speak to me. That you just came in the door."

"I did. Ask my wife. No, leave her out of it. I just came through and that's what I did."

"Forget it. How much you give Kelly so I know when I ask him for it?"

"You know, you really came out sooner than anybody and that cop expected you to. I'm not kidding when I said I spoke to him. Maybe you weren't hurt that bad after all."

"I came out because I was afraid to stay in. My head still kills me. Now how much?"

"One twenty-one and change. Fifty cents to be exact if I remember. Yeah."

"What? I had two hundred minimum between the register, tip glass and spillover box. What're you pulling on me?"

"That's all there was. I knew I shouldn't have taken the job. People always accuse you."

"Damn right. Where's the rest, Hector?"

"Where's what? I did you a favor, now you're insulting me for the lousy fifteen you gave me and all your stinking free drinks and crummy food for two days? Screw off, I'm never coming around your place," and hangs up.

I call back. "Hector please."

"Out for good, fuck you, take a walk, who you think you are?" his wife says and hangs up.

I go to bed. Trying to find a place to rest my head keeps me up half the night. Next day I go to Kelly's and he slaps his cheek when I walk in and says "God in heaven, what happened to you?"

"Looks good, huh? You didn't hear?"

"Hear? I knew something had to be wrong when I called your bar over and over again."

"It's been closed, you didn't know?"

"Nobody told. And I never leave here except back and forth home to the subways and your place isn't on my way. I thought you were sick, your heart, the insides, something that knocked you out for the first time in your life—the flu—but nothing so bad as this. What, you got hit by a truck?''

"Pipe truck. In the night, no headlights. Actually headlights —mine, but forget it, I'm still a little screwy up there. Though I'm sure it was one of Stovin's who did it, a fellow cellmate, forget the details for now, I'm tired of telling them, but just came in for my money or what Hector left of it."

"First a drink. Rye, right?''

"Can't. I'm on medication, and it's scotch.''

"Medication nonsense. Have a drink. I'll go one with you.''
He pours us both a shot and soda backup, fills a bowl with salted peanuts and puts it between us.

"What is it, Kelly? I got to go to work.''

"In your condition? Drink up, have a nut.''

"Yes to work. Now what is it, stop dillying.''

"You won't like this and which was why I was calling you over and over so much, but something funny happened to your dough. Not funny to laugh at, for you see—''

"You don't have it?''

"First listen. Drink up, have a nut.''

"Just tell me.''

"I put it away as Hector said you told me to. In my least obvious spot, nobody but me and a somebody very dear to me who wouldn't take a toothpick off the bar without first asking me, if she knew I didn't want her to. When next day, along with my own cash numbered in the hundreds which I always keep, as you also must, for Sundays and bankless holiday Mondays that we forget are coming, and all the money, yours included, was gone from the hiding spot. I couldn't believe it.''

"Hey, now wait a minute.''

"Truer than anything. Don't get excited. I was so depressed, not just for mine but much more for yours because I was holding it, that I cried right here—a couple customers, Tom, Brian—you don't know them but they'll vouch for me for that, who saw me walk from upstairs with real tears on my face.

They asked what happened. They thought a death in the family
I just heard on the phone. I knew I wasn't at fault for you but
felt that awful for—"

"Hey hey now, wait—"

"My safest place, Shaney. Locked gate in the back two
inches thick as I got, they instead went through the back
window."

"I have to sit down."

"Yes, do, sit, take a load off. Have another drink." He
pours, I wave the drink away. "Go on, go on. I'm sure,"
holding the glass to my lips and I take it from him and drink,
"I'm sure you shouldn't even be up with that injury. But you
are, so okay, you're here, so I'll tell the story, the whole. They
got in the bathroom window, must've been a kid who wormed
through the small space the bent bars made and then dodged
around the alarm traps I had set up all over the place and probably passed outside a couple-dozen bottles of my best scotch.
Because they're gone too, so I took even a worse beating than I
said. How he knew where my hiding spot was, because nobody
told him, or a she—well, some people are just smarter than me.
So what can I say but we both lucked out, though with all the
trouble you already got you have to take this much worse than
me."

"Suppose I say I don't know if I believe you?"

"Then I'd say why not?"

"Why not because maybe now that Stovin carts for you
you're also in with them some way and let them persuade you
to say the money was stolen because they want me to know
through you that things will only get worse for me for still going
against them and then beating up their friend."

"Then I'd say you must be a jerk."

"Let's see the bent bars."

"They're repaired. Think I wanted them coming back the
next night?"

"Who repaired them?"

"A craftsman. Someone I know. I'm not letting you bother

him because that part's none of your business or his."

"You reported it?"

"Sure I did. How else can I get my legal theft insurance and also put the loss plus all the other unstolen things I declared stolen on my income tax form?"

"Well, I do believe you and I don't."

"Then to me you're still a jerk. I'm your friend. Though we don't see each other twice a year, we know how hard we work and our fathers go back in this trade ages ago for years, so think I'd choose those thieves over you?"

"You did to pick up your trash."

"That was them over Ecomolos, not you."

"If you're my friend, forget the money. Just go along with me and tell whatever officials need to hear it to stop Stovin's about how they pushed the garbage pickup in our faces like dung."

"I go only so far for friendship as I do for being Mr. Easy Touch behind the bar and then, like I know you must, I stop. My life, that's first. My business, second. You want to switch them around, that's your business, your life. But now you better believe I was robbed also because if you don't then I can't talk to you again like this like friends. And why you so worried? You'll come out ahead on the robbery too. Like me tell the income tax people I was holding a couple-thousand for you and I'll back your every word."

"How much of mine you report missing?"

"I was smart for you. I only told them a big roll and why."

"No, I'll tell them the hundred-thirty or so Hector said he left. I'm strictly by the books."

"Even when you can't be insured for it?"

"Even."

"Then maybe you really are a jerk or your head got hit worse than it looks. But I got a lot of bookwork and setup to do, so what do you say we shake friendly and part solid old pals?"

We shake. I go. It's cold with another inch of snow on the ground. I flip up my collar, take out my flop hat. I bought it today three sizes too large for me regularly. It's the only size that can both protect and be set lightly on my head. Every now and then for the past day the wound bleeds through the bandage and I change it myself. The stitches are still in though the doctor promises they'll evaporate. My head still aches, probably because I don't take all the pills I'm supposed to. I don't want to get so groggy with them where I can't work or will slip on the little spilt water that's always on the bar slats, try as I might to keep that area dry, and get hurt even worse. Maybe I shouldn't go to work. No, I know I shouldn't but I have to make money because if I don't I won't have any. And I also don't want to just stay in my hotel room alone with nothing else to do but drink, which I never liked that much and along with it just to pass out or think, though with all the booze I own it's probably the one thing I can afford to.

So I open up. Place looks in okay shape. Nothing much missing: some soda, several fingers of scotch. Two minutes after I'm there someone barges in, runs to the john and I get so scared at this man throwing open the door and running past me that I drop my broom and back up against the liquor shelf and knock a bottle over, catching it as it falls. He comes back, sits on a stool, says "Beer, Shaney me boy, and I'm in a rush." I draw a beer, he puts a dollar down, looks at me and says "How's it going?"

"Fine."

"Haven't seen you open for days."

"Been away."

"Vacation?"

"No," and I give him change and go about my business. He orders another beer and when I give it to him he stares at me and says "You know, I only now noticed. What's wrong with your head? Trip on your stairs, get mugged?"

"Sort of. I don't want to go into it."

"Don't. You're not married, right?"

"No."

"I am. So I thought, well, it happens, I'm not saying it does to me, but what happened with you?''

"I really don't want to go into it, Curtis, mind?''

"No. We all have our troubles. I don't tell you mine, you don't to me yours. If I did, but you don't want to go into it. But if I did it'd be traditional—customer: bartender, not bartender to customer. Not that I'm not interested in what might have happened to you, but we'll forget it. I will. I'm sure with that face pain on your face and bandage, you can't. I'm sorry. I can't keep my mouth quiet. Tell me to shut up, tell me to go, even, if I continue to talk about it. But I think my problem is I'm too overconcerned with people's problems. This ridiculous social consciousness in me. Chasing kids down the street who rob old ladies, which some people might not find a problem of mine. The old ladies, I mean, but forget it. I'm sure it's a sick need in me, a compulsion, I'm sure. Like I wasn't a good little boy and am overcompensating for it now, but that's not what I wasn't. So I have to look after everybody and have all these ethical even religious ideals when I probably deep down don't and hate people. But give me a last one quick. I'm in a rush and talked too much.'' I do, he drinks, stands, says "Do me a favor. And I'm sorry, you're going to dislike me for sounding so well-meaning when I just admitted I'm probably really not, but take care of that head,'' and goes.

Sanitation inspector comes in and says "Chief's driving around today, Shaney, so shovel the snow from your front or I'll have to write out a summons.''

"I'll do it now. Have a beer.''

"The chief inspector.''

"Just shoot it down. What can he see from a car and my window isn't even clean.''

He sits. "I'm afraid to ask, but what happened to your head?'' I give him a beer and a bag of peanuts. He never pays for them though sometimes he tries. It's not for favors from him, which are so small as to be almost just neighborly, but because he's on his feet all day and deserves a break like any public servant patrolling the streets and keeping the law and order of things.

"Shaney, can you hear me in there? What happened to your head or don't you want to say?"

"Garbage happened to my head. You know garbage so you know how it can come from nowhere sometimes and hit your head. A brick filled with it—a private one—but maybe the less said of it the better for me and quicker the garbage brick hitters will go away."

"I don't understand you but do that you don't want to talk about it, so okay."

I give him another beer, get my shovel, go outside and clean the sidewalk of snow, throw rock salt, come back, dishwash, pour, mix, cook, make sandwiches, drinks, tap a keg, fill a three-pound coffee can with grill grease, pack two huge plastic barrels with whole liquor bottles I'm by law supposed to first break and cover them with kitchen scraps, clean out the toilets and urinals, mop the washrooms and bar floors, scour the refrigerators inside and out, dust every bottle on the bar, place phone orders for food, beer, liquor, soft drinks and different kitchen and bar accessories for the coming weeks, stock the deliveries that come in, do some accounting, pay my bills, send out laundry, work like this for only ten hours today.

I'm tired through most of the day and at midnight I shoo everybody out early but one regular who says when he's about to step out the door "Need some help, Shaney?" and I say "Nah, I can do it myself," and he says "What are you talking —you can't handle those big cans," and I say "I don't know— sure, if you can manage it, as I'm really feeling too weak to and the garbage has already been here three days."

After Al carries the barrels out he says "Worth a shot of gin, isn't it?" and I say "Think I'd've let you if it wasn't?" and he says "Not that I wouldn't have done it for you for nothing the way you're banged up," and I say "Don't worry, nobody does anything for me for nothing, just enjoy," and pour a double gin for him and he says "Can you also spare a split of ginger ale with a lime twist in it?" and I say "For sure."

64

I leave the bar with him, look around when I step outside and lock up to see nobody's going to suddenly run up and throw something at or jump on me. I ask Al to walk me home "so if I do drop dead along the way someone will be there to take me to my grave," though what I really want him for is sort of as protection. We walk, he talks. About his lost job, kids, sports, ex-sonofabitch boss, too-slim wife, funny and sexy TV shows, films and dinners he wishes he'd the money to go to and how I really shouldn't come in tomorrow with my head wrapped like so, though he guesses I probably know best what I'm doing for myself or at least better than he.

"Yes."

"If you want, give me your keys and I'll open up. I've tended bar quarter of my life and you can come in when you like."

"No thanks."

"Bar's a bar. Beer goes, I know how to tap. And I never drank a drink till six any day but my folks' funeral, God's word."

"It's not that."

"Six in the evening and by drinking I mean alcohol."

"So I thought."

"Then what? It's references, I can get. Because I'm only thinking of you and your head and of course a few bucks off the books for me."

"I'm okay."

"You're okay? You're not okay."

"What can I say? I'll survive."

"Then if you want I can take your garbage out every night and walk you home this way till you don't need me, my only pay maybe a couple double-gins on the side and coin or two just to get me home, all right?"

"Fine."

"Great. —This walking. It's so strange for me. All the years I know you—maybe a dozen—and never seen you once out of your bar, even by accident on the street."

"I know."

"I'm being truthful, not diddling with you. You're all right. You're well liked. You've been generous and more kind than all the other bars around and that's why drinkers will always go to you even if your prices are a bit high."

"Mine?"

"The Manor House for instance on G."

"All the Manor Houses are dives with the worst pimps, hookers and sprawled-out crazies and drunks in them and over-smoky, dirty and unhealthy beyond belief and wouldn't give you credit for a beer on your birthday if you showed them the birth certificate where the exact same time you asked for credit was the exact same time fifty years ago you were born. And far as their food and one on the house is concerned—well I don't know. Maybe their food's good, mine's not so hot."

"And they give free drinks."

"One after every three like me?"

"Their ratio might be lower, but believe me—"

"Pour as tall a glass and not in your big hollowed-out bottom that I think a sin to have?"

"If you slip the barman something. As to the hollow bottom, I'd have to inspect, as I didn't even know yours wasn't. But believe me, nobody I know lays a bad word on you except maybe if they're gassed."

"Why you telling me all this?"

"Like I said, to show you're liked."

"No, people always have other reasons."

"Not me. It's the truth with proof. I thought with your head hurt you needed encouragement and to know good feelings come your way from people too."

"Thanks."

"Welcome. Look, I don't mean to get personal now that I feel we know each other better. But head injury aside, I've never seen you with no smiles like this. What actually happened? Someone said something about garbage and I said 'He got slugged over that?' "

"I didn't, thanks again and I'll see you," as we're at my hotel.

"Tomorrow. You closing same time as tonight till the bandages come off?"

"Earlier."

"I'll be in before then. Ten. Help you around, sweep up, do that—pots even. I draw the line at toilets, at least inside them unless you pay me real well, and take out your garbage and see you to home. Still on?"

"Sure."

We shake, I go in, not expecting to see him tomorrow because what drinkers promise the night before are like light-years away in memory the next day, check for messages, are none, wonder if Stovin's is through with me figuring as I do that we're all squared up now: one of each of us landing in the hospital and me with several forever lost workdays. If they let me alone from now on I won't broadcast to the world what went on between us anymore. They wouldn't want me to, thinking other storeowners they want to do or do garbage business with might get similar ideas and defy them or try to which Stovin's might hold me responsible for starting it all. I just want to get better and find an apartment and work and do business the way I've always done it: alone with the tradesmen I want to do it with.

A telegram's under my door. No name on it, just my hotel address and room number and the message says "Nice and quiet now huh?"

I go downstairs and ask the nightclerk "How'd I get this?"

"Telegraph people. Wanted to phone it in and when you didn't answer, delivered it by hand."

"How come it wasn't in my box?"

"Telegrams we think are important messages, and since people are inclined to rob from boxes when we're not looking, we stick them under your door."

"If it's so important why wasn't it pushed all the way into my room instead of hanging half outside into the hall?"

"Boy who pushed it didn't do his job. In any case we got it away from downstairs."

"And there's no name on it, just the room. Why you so sure it was for me?"

"That's your room number, four-twenty, so that's you."

"But I've only been in my new room for two days. It could've been meant for the guest right before me."

"Let's see, last before you," and he looks in the register. "Oh yeah, a couple not even for the night. Two men, they gave fake names, passing themselves off in the afternoon as a father and son team in for a funeral and needing a few hours repose."

"Then for them then: 'Nice and quiet now huh?' Maybe their friends knew they were here and it was some kind of occasion like a celebration for the two men and the message was an odd inside joke that that group likes to play."

"If their friends knew they were here for only the big honeymoon day, why would they send it two days late? Besides that it's not how it was. Those two were right out of a goldfisted mensroom. That telegram had to be meant for you."

"Who was in my room before the men?"

"I can't even give that information to the police."

"Sure you can. Police come in my bar all day long and tell me how they operate."

"This telegram really worries you, nice almost peaceful-like message and all?"

"For my own reasons, yes."

"Tied to those bizarre early morning phonecalls you used to get? No? Well, if you have to know who was before you not counting our honeymooners, something I don't do for everyone I want you to know. It's illegal, but seeing you have to relieve your mind some, I suppose I can bend the law backwards a little—"

"You drink, don't you?"

"I don't go psycho on rum but do enjoy the taste of it."

"Tomorrow I'll bring a bottle of my best stuff if you want."

"I won't complain." Looks in the register. "Not worth

two?''

"For a name? All right, two."

"Second one you could make it cheap or even both. Anyway, you now know you can call on me for other things. —Of course, the elderly gentleman, Mr. Addissay, no help to you I'm afraid, who lived here as a permanent for six years. I wasn't supposed to tell you this, bad luck and even worse hotel business, since nobody likes to know he's sleeping in the same bed and bedroom someone recently died in, though I suspect you've seen and heard it all. He actually only had a rough time the last few days there and passed away on the stretcher going downstairs."

"That doesn't bother me. The honeymooning couple does more."

"Way to go. Though I for one have nothing against them no matter how they mutilate their bodies, unless they're truly taking advantage of the very young."

Telegram could still be a mistake. That's what I'll think: not from Stovin's to me but meant for 419 or 421 or even 520 or something, and just get a good night's sleep.

Little later I call the telegraph office and a man says "Room number and address is correct but telegram was sent from another city and sender gave an anonymous."

I have a couple of drinks in my room, try to sleep, still staying away from most of the pills I'm to take, particularly since I'm drinking, and can't sleep and then oversleep and awake, eat, walk to work with an even worse headache than yesterday's and knowing I should take a cab, but on that score I've always been a cheapskate. All my bar garbage is on the sidewalk where we left it the night before.

I call George Ecomolos and tell him about the garbage and say "What's the trouble—you got a strike or something?"

"Worse than that, but think on the phone I be telling you, you're nuts."

"Come on then. It's cold and I'll heat up a bad brandy for you," and he says "Come around again your place I got to be doubly nuts than I just said before. Talking to you now even I'm nuts and so shouldn't. I will though, talk. They go so far to bother you and me with taps, they nuts.''

"Who?''

"Who? Ha. That's who. You nuts or stupid or both those two? The name. Our private garbage pals, your friends and mine. They phonecall me, understand? And say deal off to buy my trash trucks if. If what if what I say and they say to me back not to pick your garbage up anytime now. If I do they don't buy my trucks and make sure nobody does and on that threat I think they win and if they do I be all the way out to space and broke. Okay, I told and hope they not be tapping. You say one word though—oh hell, should have said nothing to you, nothing, for now I worry.''

"It's all right. I won't tell anyone.''

"It's not. People shoot off mouths. Best of them shoot off— my wife, God bless her, everybody, not purposely, a disease. But they really into you, Shaney. Maybe next only to squeeze you slow-wise where you got garbage piled miles high. I hope not. City stinks like it is. But boy they got ways nobody does and when they tell very firmly me lay off, Eco, I must. Hey, I see you, baby, and swear has to be last time for a year everything me to you sight and sound, so so long.''

I call most of the private carting companies in the city and each tells me he can't pick up my garbage because that's Eco's territory. I tell them Eco's going out of business and they say something like "That so? Didn't know. What happened?'' and I say "I think Eco himself got sick of the city or something or just sick. But Stovin's who's taking over Eco's customers won't handle me,'' and I get answers like "Maybe they've good reasons. . . . Eco might have told Stovin you don't pay your bills, so why should we chance it?. . . That's their concern and much as I'd like to and can always use the extra cash coming in and thank you for thinking of me, I can't, sorry,'' and a few of them just say "Sorry'' right after I tell them Stovin's won't handle me, and hang up.

I bring the filled garbage bags to the basement and carry the loose garbage in boxes to a corner trashcan a block away. What I carry is about a tenth of my garbage and fills up a whole city can. While I'm jamming it into the can a man says "You shouldn't be doing that. That's for public trash alone."

"I know and I'm sorry but must."

"Then if you know, stop, please, have some civic pride and decency. Take what you put in out and put it in the cans in front of buildings or stores where it belongs. Continue stuffing it in, mister, and you're in trouble."

"You're right, sorry again," and I walk away with some of my trash and stick it in a public can on the next corner a block away. Same man's there when I turn around and he says "Now I warned you. Two times in two minutes is too much in one day. What's your name? I'm calling a cop."

"James Blackmore. I've nothing to hide. I live in that building there, second floor, window with the flowerbox is mine. All our cans were filled so this is what I was forced to do to both get the smells out of my apartment and keep the sidewalk clean," and I cross the street, go in the building I said was mine, through the vestibule door watch the man look around for someone or maybe he was just faking me. Anyway, no cop comes and he looks up to what I said was my window, gives one of those disgusted looks and walks away. I go back to the bar, serve customers, an hour later lock up and return to the first trashcan with two boxes of empty condiment bottles, a big roastbeef bone and broken barware and such. When I get back to the bar I'm beat and have to take a few aspirins and rest for an hour on two chairs. Then I open up again. At least I got rid of the loose heavier trash and broken glass that would've ripped the bags. Later I'll think of ways more.

Most regulars stop asking after my head and start bitching I'm too slow. "My manager's coming back to the shoestore in a minute, Shaney. Bad head and all and much as I sympathize for you, try and hustle it up?" I try to as I want to keep them but it's tough.

Al comes around eleven, does some odd jobs for me and then I close up and we carry several plastic garbage bags to the first trashcan I was at this morning. It's gone, though my boxes with trash are still there, and we at my suggestion start walking to the trashcan a block further away when he says "Why not just put them in front of any building with garbage?"

"Good idea. My head hasn't been thinking the same since it got hit," and we leave the bags in front of some buildings.

Back at the bar I give him a couple of bucks and drinks and have one with him with more aspirins and while he walks me to my hotel he says "Ever think of selling the bar, with all the problems you got with it?" and I say "What would I do if I did?"

"Bake in the sun down south someplace or on one of those tropical foreign isles or keys."

"And after the first day with a burnt-up back, to do what?"

"Apply lotion to it, rest off the burn and get a new one a week later."

"And after that and after that? That's what I'm saying."

"Golf, fish, swim, sail, tennis or learn any or all of them. Or meet a young lady or one closer your own age, but get laid, gamble, play the ponies, eat well and drink."

"Oh fun fun fun and after the first month of dying of boredom or liver disease, what?"

"Open a bar down there and call it Shaney's."

"I don't know anyone there at any of those places. All my customers and what you might call friends are here. I'm a city boy, born, raised and worked here almost all my life, even if that is a city under the southern sun you're talking of where you want me to be. Worse, I don't like that much sand, sun and palm trees or really any trees. I like them in the park, even if I only get to see them if I go out of my way when I walk to work. Also pavement, sidewalk, whatever the hell materials the streets are made of I mean. But real life, seasons, snow and getting snowed on and trudging through drifts and shoveling it if I'm not sick like this. And biting rains, freezing colds, noise, lots of noise, a madhouse, old and new tall buildings going up and torn down, car and people congestions and rushes—even grimy streets in a way if they don't get too unclean. Besides, my memories are all here—my parents' and sister's graves."

"I didn't know you had sisters."

"One. Long ago. Maybe nobody does. We were very close. She died when I was a kid, but I remember her."

"Then come visit them once a year to pay your respects and lay flowers. With a jet and cab you can probably be at the gravesite in three hours."

"Who'll take care of my southern or foreign bar?"

"An assistant. Someone you know who can make drinks and sandwiches and trust."

"You must be the only regular left I didn't tell this yet. I never had an assistant who didn't steal me blue in the face and blind. They've always been one step ahead of me and I also want everything to be run exactly my way, so I'm a lousy boss."

"So I'll come down and work for you and won't steal and I know the business and got nothing to gain standing here and my wife can wait your tables."

"I told you about Stovin's?"

"All I need to know I suppose or so you thought."

"What I say? I forget—my head."

"All that you didn't want to do what they wanted you to and for it you got brained."

"Then you can see why should I be so sure you're not working for them too? Trying to get me to sell out cheap and save them the inconvenience of beating my butt in again and maybe this time one of them getting caught with no excuse."

"Hey. You know me how long before you ever heard their name, so I can almost take what you say as an insult."

"I've got to be extra careful."

"It could still be one."

"I'm sorry but so far it's not in me to rely on any one person I know."

"I'm what I say I am, honestly. Total your register, work out whatever shadowing system you have, then put me behind the bar for as long as you like and you'll see. Not a penny will slip into my pocket that's not a tip for me and even that if you don't want it to and my wife is even worse."

"Anyway, nobody will buy my bar except for the oldtime fixtures and liquor stock, so how can I invest in any place new? I just have to stick at what I still got."

"Here's your hotel. You were going to walk past. Hey, these talks have been swell," and we shake hands.

"Al, I'm kind of sorry I never spoke to you as much before. But maybe, as you know, if you did work behind a bar—"

"I did, what are you going on for?"

"Then you know that after a while almost everyone on the other side of the bar gets to look and act alike to you, but you're all right."

"I don't know. Working the bar even twelve hours straight never turned me off to people or them to me."

"You're lucky. Goodnight," and I go inside. "How you doing?" I say to the nightclerk and he says "What's this? You haven't my bottles? That a way to treat your helpmate?"

"Damn it, I forgot," and give him five dollars.

"What's this? Bribery now?" Puts it back in my hand. "Bottles, not money. Two quarts like you promised and it'll be worth twice as much to me as that five."

"Tomorrow."

Next day under my bar's front door is a summons from the Sanitation Department for leaving trash on the street. I phone the Department's summons section and say "What trash where did I leave? My sidewalk was clean when I left it last night and clean today."

"Inspector's report says you left it in front of private dwellings and storefronts not your own."

"What? Streets as dirty as they are and sidewalks with ice and still unshoveled snow on them for people to fall and this inspector has the time to untie every trash bag in town to see what's inside really belongs to the people in the building it's in front of?''

"Our office got a phonecall."

"Who from?"

"Someone. Maybe a landlord or storeowner, maybe a passing citizen. In such complaints when you're so completely infringing on the law, the courts say you don't have to know who are your accusers. Want a hearing, I'll put you down for one. You'll have to pay your fine first, which you'll get back with interest if you win, though next June do you? For that's how far we're backed up. But from now on if you can't afford private carters, don't go leaving envelopes and things with your name and address on them in the bags you leave at places where you shouldn't."

"Many thanks."

"For what?" and hangs up.

That night Al and I rip up all the address labels and bill envelopes and stuff before sticking them in with the rest of the garbage and distribute the trash bags and garbage cartons in front of buildings and stores three and four blocks from the bar. When we get back I give him a few bucks, tell him to help himself behind the bar and pour me a tall scotch with rocks, lock up and he walks me to the hotel and says looking at the sky "Nicer night tonight isn't it?" and I say "They're all the same."

"All the same? Stars, planes, moon with rings around it when you couldn't see anything but clouds last night?" and I say "All right, tonight's different."

"How's your head getting?—that's what I should've asked before, forget the stars and night," and I say "Better."

"You're not talkative tonight, I won't," and I say "No, I like to, takes my mind away, great night, oh yes, great night."

"You've new troubles?" and I say "Who said I had troubles in the first place?"

"When's the bandage finally coming off?" and I say "Maybe when I see a doctor, which might be never. No coverage, that's why I don't like going to them so much."

"Want my wife to look at it and patch you up again? She once had some practical nursing training and has done it for me," and I say "That might be nice."

"Or a clinic. Maybe you should just go to one," and I say "They'll hear I own a bar and make me pay them regular overpriced fees till I'm bankrupted."

"Don't pay them," and I say "Hospitals it's not in me to welsh on so long as I got."

"But it could be getting infected from whatever aftereffects and your neglecting it," and I say "If it was I'd feel it with a fever and more pain than a pounding headache, so if your wife would, I'd like you to ask."

"First thing when I get home if she's not asleep. But three nights in a row, Shaney. You could almost call mine permanent work for you after what I've had the last few months," and I say "Actually if it continues working out like this, I probably could put you on evenings seven to twelve starting around Monday so you could really make some dough and I could both open up and go home sooner. For the time being I think I need to."

"Great," and I say "Favor for a favor—okay, settled and maybe, if you're as honest as you say, all day Sunday if you can and without my even coming and leaving there," and we reach the hotel and shake hands and he seems happy and slaps my back and says "Sorry, slapped it too hard it looks like," and I say "Little, it hurt my head but I'll survive," and we say goodnight.

"Oh Jesus, the bottles," to the nightclerk and he says "You know, one more round of your amnesia and I'm going to start letting those early morning calls to you through."

"I still get them?"

"Occasionally, in various male and female voices, that they just have to absolutely speak to you—it's that important."

"Tomorrow definitely, the best stuff I have—even three."

"Don't overdo to the degree where you could then think it's worth it to forget again. Two regular-sized rums will suit me fine."

Next morning on my way to work I make a point of walking past the park to see the snow inside. It's still clean and relatively untrampled in and from the border wall I see a dog leaping in it. I also see a rabbit, second time here in my life, and two boys, probably cutting school, sledding down a hill. When they see me looking at them I wave and yell "Hiya doing, fellas?" and they yell "Hi, come on in, water's fine," while they wave back.

There's no Sanitation summons waiting for me at the bar so so far so good today. Business is the same as usual, but since the weather's much colder and it's snowed a little more and walking for everyone's slippery going, that could be a positive sign. Al comes at ten with his wife and she looks at my head and from her kit treats and repatches it better than the doctor did, while Al cleans up, restocks the bar, taps a keg and gets rid of the garbage by himself somewhere outside. His wife's funny and sweet, over drinks I provide they tell me about their kids and married life, when they walk me to my hotel I ask Al to come to work as a bartender tomorrow at seven and he shouts "Hurray" and they embrace and Tina hugs me.

I go inside and give the nightclerk a shopping bag. He pulls one of the bottles out, looks at the label and says "This is the best rum there is. You shouldn't have gone this far, even if I'm not saying do it again and I won't be your friend," and gives me a fresh copy of tomorrow morning's newspaper and for the first time says "Have a pleasant sleep."

Al comes every day on time, does a good job, makes even more at the bar and with the food than I did in the same period a week ago. All the customers think he's a find and from what I can see he doesn't steal a dime from me nor drink on the job or keep the place anything but clean and he gets rid of all the garbage every night without my getting one summons. With him working the night shift alone and me the days, I not only get to rest my head a lot more but net more in a week than I usually do including his pay. On Friday and Saturday nights and all day Sunday, when I take my first real day-off since I took over the place and just stay in the hotel and read the papers and sleep, Tina works with him, cooking and waiting tables just for the tips in it and for what sandwiches she can bring home to her kids and says she earns enough and in food to make it more than worthwhile for herself. I later tell Al "Next Sunday and any night you and Tina are here, save a little on the babysitter if you want and have your kids come in for supper on me."

About two weeks after Al starts bartending for me, he doesn't show up. I call him at home but nobody answers. I wait till ten o'clock and then a little unused to working so many hours in one day I say "Last call, everyone," and stick the garbage in trash bags and bring them to the basement. A lot of customers are disappointed Al didn't show, but I tell them he's probably sick or maybe had to suddenly fly to a sick parent or his wife's someplace and he'll be in tomorrow or the next day. I lock up and take a cab to my hotel, as this time so late at night I'm still too scared with my head still in bad shape to walk home alone.

I call Al next morning and say "Where were you?" and he says "I'm really sorry, Shaney, but can't say."

"Why, you were sick or something bad with your wife and kids?"

"I won't say, I should've put it like that. That way I didn't say anything, neither no or yes, so it's silly of you to guess."

"It's Stovin's."

"Did I say?"

"Just by your voice I know they got to you."

"I'm afraid what you know is nothing, not that I mean to be mean to you over the phone. You've been good to us and I appreciate it."

"Then continue coming in."

"I can't."

"I've really gotten used to you. You even have the job after I get well."

"I can't."

"Even Tina, who on weekend nights and Sunday I'll pay."

"We'd like to but can't."

78

"Why?"

"You know I won't say."

"Then give me a hint. Blink once for yes if it's Stovin's who's stopping you and twice for it isn't."

"How will that help you?"

"You mean if I knew?"

"I mean in my blinking over a telephone, but that too: if you knew."

"Oh, I got one of those old videophones installed last night, didn't you know? I can see everything to everyone I dial to but they can't see me back."

"Sure you do. Me too. I can see you right now lying and crying your ass off. But again, how would it help you if you knew?"

"Knew what?"

"You joking me?"

"No, I'll be honest, I forgot."

"Your head's really in first-rate remembering powers today. If I was you I'd see a doctor fast. Knew who it was I was saying —not that it was anybody or anything except my not wanting to continue working for you because you're a little tightfisted. You also drive me too hard and I don't like the way you treat my wife and also that I got a much better job."

"All that's bull and you know it. And who'd hire you except someone desperate as me?"

"A bar. Nicer and cleaner place and which pays better and longer hours. I'm not saying where so you can call up and say lying things to fire me. But how would it help you if you knew?"

"Knew it was Stovin's who got you to quit? Why you so interested in knowing? They also ask you to find out my next moves?"

"I'm not interested, see ya."

"Hold it. It would first of all prove my first impressions of you when you were just a customer and make me think I'm thinking right and true again and that's that you're a fucking scumbag and rat who'd screw anyone in the back for a few bucks and drinks the first time someone asked.''

"Sure I am. That's what I did. Boy, you know me better than my wife. I only wish she had a second chance to take care of your head. This time I'd show her how.''

"Don't come in my bar anymore, weakling.''

"Why should I? You're crazy and a liar. Besides, I got my own now,'' and hangs up.

I slam the receiver down. "You bastard,'' I shout.

Customer looks up at me. "What's wrong? One of the guys you give credit here gave you a check and his bank won't honor it?''

"You have a job?''

"Yeah I have a job. What's it to you the personal questions? I pay, don't I?''

"I thought you might like to help me out with my garbage tonight if you didn't.''

"Garbage? Me? In these clothes?''

"For after.''

"For after I put on even better clothes.''

"Know anyone who'd like that kind of work? Just for an hour or two six nights a week and good for a couple of bills and free drinks and eats.''

"If I hear of anyone I'll let him know.''

"No, forget it. Next person I get to help me will screw me even worse.''

"Uh, no offense, but that's your attitude not to trust anyone, who'd be dumb enough to come here to work?''

"Shut up. Have another on me.''

"Eat shit, Fleet. I need your lip too?'' and slaps a bill down and starts out.

"I didn't mean to 'shut up' like I meant it. I meant it to mean—'' Hell, he's gone. It's partly my head. Has to be. It's all excitable. Maybe something festering in there. I've had headaches all week. I don't take care of myself well. I don't want to be in more pain and die. When my time comes, okay, but not from my stupidity in not doing anything about it when I could. Maybe Tina did something to it she knew would slowly make it worse. No, that's not nice, she was all right. What should I do? I pour a drink. No, that's not it, and I put it down without a sip. Do something sensible, that's what. Customer comes in. I say "Closed."

"Closed when the door's open and place is freezing inside? Now it's closed," and he shuts the door.

"Last customer left it like that when he left. But closed. I got to get to the hospital. What are you, you look like one, a cabby?"

"I'm off duty now. All I came in for was a burger and beer."

"But my head. I'll get my coat on and give you a good tip. Hospital's not that far."

"Really, it's not the money. I'm bushed, six hours straight on the streets, I have to sit and be quiet and eat."

"But you can see what kind of shape. I got hit. Long ago but haven't paid much attention to it. I think I could be dying with a brain clot for all I know."

"You're not dying, it's just all of a sudden you're scared you are. You'll be fine. There are plenty of available cabs. I'll go some other place for my break and see you another day. Lots of luck to you, friend."

He leaves and I lock up and call a cab and go to the emergency section of the hospital. I see a doctor and after some neurological nose-touching and barefoot walking she says I have the headachy remains of a concussion and a slight infection and gives me a prescription for it, repatches me with a small bandage and that's that. "Stay off your feet for a week and don't take any alcohol with your pills and you'll live."

"I have to work."

"Then work less, nothing fatiguing, but you're in no danger and practically healed."

I get the prescription filled, take a couple of pills, have a soup at a shop and go back to the bar. I feel relieved and even stronger now and my headache's almost gone. I even look better, looking in the bar mirror: at least the hat when I wear it outside covers all the bandages now and doesn't make me look so dumb anymore. And without the hat my whole forehead and top of my hairline now shows and I can comb some of the hair over the patch, though being thin and wavy it never stays and I was warned not to wet my hair and slick it back as the patch and tape have to stay dry.

That night I unidentify all my garbage, stick it in several trash bags and tell my customers before I close that the next drink or a grilled cheese sandwich is free if they take a bag each with them when they leave and drop it only where there are other trash bags and cans legally placed. A few customers take me up on it and I put the rest of the bags and cartons of garbage in the basement where I already have a stack of them.

Morning following the third night I do this and when I'm just about getting rid of all my garbage this way, I find five big trash bags in front of my bar and under my door a summons for leaving these bags on the street overnight. I didn't think I could get away with getting rid of my garbage forever like this but I hoped I could till I thought of a longer-lasting plan. I look in the bags and see none of them are mine. The name of the inspector I know is on the summons, as it wasn't on the last one I got, and I phone him, he's not in and much later in the day he calls me back.

"Mr. Fleet?"

"Mr. Fleet? Shaney. That garbage you gave me a summons for, Dolph, isn't mine. Some group, and I know whose, put the bags there just to intimidate me more than they've done for the last couple of months."

"You read the papers?"

"When I've time."

"If you read it every day you'd know my reason for not skipping you over this morning, or at least before I spoke to you about it, and also why I have to get tough with your sidewalk snow. There's been charges, maybe some that are founded also, besides hidden-camera photos showing corruption going right to the top of our department. That's why everybody has to do his extra effort to prove it's not true and even no small spotlight falls on him or his brass, understand?''

''All I'm saying is that garbage wasn't mine. No corruption, no payoffs, none of those.''

''Okay. Say I'm talking as though I never knew you, why should my section assume it wasn't your garbage in front of your bar when it was clearly in front of your bar and garbage?''

''Because I looked in those bags I got a summons for. It's not bar trash. No twenty squeezed lemons and limes or long sandwich bread bags or empty gallon salad oil cans or a thousand cigarette butts and maraschino cherry stems. That was mostly household junk, old disposable stuff, paper diapers, breakfast cereal boxes, cat crap and banana scraps and used toothpaste tubes. But no envelopes and such identifying it as mine. One bag was even full of things that had to come from a drugstore, so it's plain someone put it in front of my bar from there.''

''The drugstore bag I can probably get the drugstore for, as that one really shouldn't be in front of your bar. But someone else's envelope could've been disposed at your bar and diapers changed when the customer and her baby were there, so could still be part of your trash.''

''And the cat crap?''

''You can distinguish between cat crap and a kid's?''

''They stink differently.''

''Listen. You know bar garbage and I know all garbage and when a cat and kid eat milk and meat they both stink the same. And what bar doesn't have a cat?''

''Mine because the city health law says I can't have loose pets lying around. But also, who'd bring in a big empty box of laundry detergent just to stick in my trash?''

''Who's to say? People are forgetful and might've forgotten on their way to your place to drop it in a street can like they intended and only realized when they got to your bar that they still had hold of it. That's happened to me, it hasn't to you? I'm not saying it's absolutely so in this particular case, but you want whys and whatfors and I can give you all of them and some. But keep the drugstore trash there and a man will come by to pick it up."

"No, I know the druggist and he's a nice guy and sometimes customer and I don't want to get him in trouble."

"Either you're a great storyteller or you're showing yourself as this over-holy martyr, but if not the drugstore then what do you want from me? For one thing, I can't do you any more favors, even tiny inconsequential ones which for the record was all they were, for things now are too hot. For a second thing, I might've just slit my throat out with all that talk now about favors and things being hot and inconsequential, because a colleague here known for her eyes said she saw some of our phones being bugged by the special anticorruption force. For I hope a final thing, if garbage is in front of your bar when it shouldn't be, then until the current scandal's over, it's your garbage and only yours. I can't be expected to inspect every trash bag to see whose it is."

"What should I do then—stay awake every night in my place to see that no one dumps garbage in front?"

"Tell me, why would they?"

"I don't want to say."

"Come on. Maybe with all my garbage knowledge I can help and even the anticorruptors bugging this phone if they are —why would they?"

"Okay. After hollering till I'm hoarse about it I kept quiet because I thought they'd go away, but it's obvious they won't. You see, for years I had the same carter. You know me so you know never a garbage or sidewalk violation from you guys except maybe a rare mistake that's one, but anyway now the old carter won't cart. A new carter wanted to and for all I know frightened the old one into not carting for me anymore. But now the new carter which wanted to cart less trash for more money, won't. They also I think think I'm going to start off like a snowball a whole slew of small stores not to throw in with them too."

"This new carter's Stovin's?"

"You heard what they've been doing to these neighborhood stores?"

"I only know them because they're the only new carter in your area, so two and two makes sense. We've heard no complaints about them."

"People are scared. I am too in a way but I don't want to commit business suicide, because this bar's my life."

"Storeowners haven't even complained that they're scared. No sign of coercion in any way do I get and I speak to them every day."

"Because they're very scared. Believe me I spoke to several of them too. They won't tell you I did because that's how scared they are. And why should I lie about this to you? There's no gain in it for me. And if I seemed crazy for a while it's because of the pipe I'm positive Stovin's put someone up to fixing my head with, but even now, even if I don't sound so sometimes, I'm pretty clear. And I don't want to tussle with them. I just want to get them off my back and someone else to cart for me."

"Who was doing it for you before?"

"Can't say. That guy could also get his pipe from Stovin's."

"You went to the police?"

"Sure. They say I've no proof."

"No proof for them's supposed to be proof for me? You can't name names, how am I to believe you?"

"When it comes between this nice company owner's life and you not believing me and my getting more summonses, which you think I'll choose?"

"Look, stop the over-holy martyring for a minute, for how my to help?"

"By just giving it. Name me one other company than Stovin's who'll cart for me."

"Hold it." He gets a list and says "For your area," and rattles the names off including Eco.

"Tried them all. None'll budge. They say it's not their area or a dozen other excuses. There's no real competition for business garbage in the city. Either one shoves the other out or together they got it portioned off.''

''First offense I never heard of. As for portioning off, that's one way of keeping the streets freer of traffic and noise during sleeping hours. But who of I mentioned before handled you—Eco? It's the only one on the list I heard's going out of business.''

''You just talk to Stovin's or any of the other carters and see why they won't handle me and I bet you learn something you didn't know before, or am I fooling myself?''

''I can't deal with them. That's private garbage, we're public. So only when rubbish blows off their trucks or they mess up the streets picking their customers' stuff up do we have any reason to squawk.''

''Then why my talking to you for? Anyway, I'll think about answering your summons and I might even call your anticorruption force. Yeah, I'll call them, maybe I'll get some satisfaction finally—know who there is in charge?''

''Read the newspapers,'' and hangs up.

I borrow a customer's newspaper. It's the better paper here, bigger so more unwieldy flipping through it, smaller runnier print, no scandal in it today, if they do have any of the others any other day, but federal: senator sentenced in influence-peddling case, ambassador called back for not paying income taxes, energy executives accused of entertaining environmental chief, vice president's administrative assistants take mistresses and boyfriends on round-the-world junkets.

Little later a man comes in selling the afternoon tabloid and I buy it. Lots of stories of city and state corruption: top judges give in-laws jobs through court, parents buying their children's way into medical and dental colleges, morticians burying cheaper coffins than they sold the bereaved, doctors collecting illegal health insurance fees, lawyers selling babies stolen from hospital incubators to childless couples out West, and way further in the paper the Sanitation scandal. While I'm reading

Dolph calls. "If you're serious about seeing the anti people, don't breathe you ever treated me to a beer, even if it was always off-hours for me and the regular free beer you give everyone after the first three. Just say I bought the first, we rolled double or nothing for the second and I won and that was my heavy drinking for the night: twice. Better yet, say I won the toss but refused the prize as one's where I draw the line. No, don't even say I was gambling, innocent dice or otherwise. I just have one beer, watch a little TV and go home."

"Don't worry. I'm known as tongue-tied Shaney for my friends."

"Where's my guarantee? Choice of saving or wrecking your business, anyone's mouth could go haywire."

I finish the article and find it's District Attorney Talven I should contact. I call, get somebody under him and say "I think I've important information on the Sanitation scandal or at least can add to it, my information can—" and he says "Listen carefully to me. Don't give your name, address or phone number unless I request it or say another unsolicited word. Our phones here have a tendency of getting disturbed. Are you presently in any personal danger?"

"I was clubbed once. Before that—"

"That's all. Next answer just a negative or yes to the question are you now on a private line?"

"At my bar."

"Please—I said negative or yes. Is yours a pay phone?"

"No."

"Good. Don't give the bar's name or if you own it or don't. Simply stay there, keep the receiver off without disconnecting us for a minimum of ten minutes and we'll trace it and come to you. Are you able to do that?"

"Yes."

"When you hear recorded music it'll mean we know where you are and are on our way and you can hang up. Anything goes wrong before then, call us back."

I leave the receiver off, twenty minutes later say into it "I didn't hear any music. Have you traced me, sir?'' Nobody answers, I repeat the question, get a dial tone and hang up. Probably better I don't meet them, seeing how they botched up just the simple task of tracing me. And our two interests really aren't related, private and public garbage and all that, so I don't call back.

A woman comes in that evening, takes a bar stool and says ''Bloody Marsky, hold the pepper, lots of vodka, Slavic style if you got and rocks.'' She looks and is dressed kind of seamy and scouts the place as if all she's interested in is who'll screw her for money or buy her drinks and preferably both. I never liked the professional pickup or freeloader in my bar. It reflects badly on me and sometimes on my father to the few oldtimers who remember him, and also makes a lot of men mad when the woman doesn't come across gratis after all those bought drinks or suddenly out of nowhere makes a phonecall, grabs her bag and goes. But you can get sued for kicking someone out for something they didn't do or they're not, so I'll just watch her.

I make her drink and say ''Dollar even, please,'' and she says ''Boy, that's cheap,'' opens her handbag, keeps it open without taking anything out and says ''I wonder if you can help me. About an hour ago I was speaking to a man on the phone here. But we were cut off and when I tried calling him back your line was busy. Anyone here keep the phone off the hook for a while around that time?''

''An hour ago? How about four?'' and she says low enough only for me to hear ''Tone it down, honey. I'm Assistant D.A. Ischgewitz, you spoke to my associate Assistant D.A. Digsby before, though don't refer to either of us as such. Jerelle. Just Jerelle, as though you know me somewhat.''

''Okay Jerelle, how you doing tonight?'' and I put my hand out to shake.

''Excuse me,'' still low, stirring her drink, ''but do you normally shake your customers' hands after you serve them their drinks?''

''Usually when they come in.''

"That's what I thought. Then why do you want to shake mine now and so ostentatiously as though you knew me well? I don't want to shake it. It's too obvious and doesn't suit my role or yours. You want to give my cover away and maybe get us both knocked off?"

"No."

"Of course not. That's it—hand down, relax, wipe the counter if you have nothing to do and your hand's itchy and it actually is a little filthy around my glass. Now, is there a possibility we can get knocked off? I have gotten my share of death threats during this investigation, though far below par."

"I've been threatened too."

"But can we immediately, in answer to my question, by anyone here?"

I look around, couple of familiar customers, wipe the bar, "No."

"All right. Now by whom before, and what Digsby said was with a club?"

"A pipe. I only said I'd been clubbed because it seemed like not the right use of language anymore to say I'd been piped. Stovin's Private Carting Company."

She sips, thinks over. "You know, this Mary merits a B plus in my humble estimation and I'm an expert on them. Pepper always poisons it."

"I don't usually put in much."

"You didn't this time, did you? Even a pinch of it is especially bad for my health."

"You said leave it out, I did."

"Who's Stovin's?"

"This bandage on my head? They also set fire to my apartment and have threatened to do much worse. Now they're dumping trash as a kind of harassment on my sidewalk and Sanitation is giving me summonses for Stovin's dirty work."

"Members of the Sanitation Department are involved in a possible collusion with this carter?"

"Not that I know of."

"Then why'd you call us? Your problem if there is one should be dealt with by investigators of private carters."

"I know. Truth is I had misgivings before and after phoning you about you coming here. I only went along with it thinking maybe you'd tip me off who to go to with my complaint, because nobody else knows."

Pushes her drink aside, looks mad. "Do you realize you've taken up two very important hours of my incredibly limited time, counting getting dressed like an idiot like this and traffic here and no doubt back? I don't know. Christ I'm pissed. Oh, start with Sergeant Lars of this precinct if he still handles extortions and rackets, but other than him—"

"He was the one in on this from the beginning. He said I had nothing going for me."

Grabs her bag, gets off the stool and starts to leave.

"You didn't pay for your Bloody Mary."

Turns to me. "Listen, barowner, don't make me angrier. I might look weak and stupid but I can pull strings."

"You want to close my place, go on and close it."

"I don't have to go that far. Just keep your cool."

"Then what? Those drinks cost money. You had a hot head before you even came in here. Taking up your time, well hell, so am I—I've got time—your stupid recorded phone music that doesn't work. And also losing my shirt because of this garbage thing and almost my head and no help from Sanitation, you or the police. And you yourself said a dollar's cheap for that drink."

"For what? You hardly put a shot in it and I hardly took a sip."

"You wear lipstick."

"Wash it off the glass with soap—soap!"

"I always do. I meant that it gets in the drink. Even if it didn't I'd still have to throw it out. That's the health law. You telling me to violate it? Actually why my getting so upset? Usually I give a police officer or anyone similar on the force or for the law a complimentary round or bite to eat if they want, just for the hard and dangerous job they have on the streets."

"I'm glad I didn't hear that," and leaves.

"Who she think she is?" a customer says.

"You helped me with a trash bag last night, want to again for another drink or grilled cheese?"

"Cheese. Little lettuce-tomato on it this time. I've drank enough and am all out of dough, even for a tip."

I make him a sandwich, give him a trash bag to get rid of someplace. Give another man a couple of beers for taking out two trash bags. First man comes back and says "If I haul away one more you'll give me a shot of cheap scotch?" I pour him one, he drinks up and starts taking the bag away. "Make it two bags for the large shot I gave," and he says "That's too much. I've a bum shoulder since I was a kid." I say "Knock off with the excuses—just take the damn two," and he does. I put the rest of the bags in the basement, phone for a cab to take me to my hotel, lock up when I see the cab coming and next day I find twice as many bags in front of the bar than the previous morning, some when I inspect inside them the same bags I gave the two customers last night, and another summons. I bring the bags downstairs, where I've a pile of about thirty now.

All morning, when I've the time to, I take some of the smaller softer garbage and break it up a little more or just flush it down the toilet as is if I think it's small enough. Around noon one of the customers comes back from the bathroom and says my toilet's backed up. I go to it. Floor's full of water and toilet paper and some of the garbage I flushed down has come back and is floating at the top of the toilet bowl with somebody's stools. I scoop the stuff out and try the plunger, but it doesn't unclog it. I mop the floor and phone a plumber. While he's in the toilet with his plumber's snake pushing the garbage to the sewer, a Department of Health inspector comes in and asks to see my basement.

"Routine?"

"More. Someone complained you have it all filled with trash and vermin."

"Who?"

"Anonymous, but the complaint slip says the caller's voice sounded sane and brainy enough to make us have to check it through."

"Sure, I got trash down there. But in plastic bags, sealed tight—they don't even smell or not much, at least not way up here. And I spray roachkiller all over them every day. You smell anything?"

"Stale beer and roachkiller, but my nose hasn't been the same for a month."

"What's the matter, a cold?"

"The season. You have schoolage kids packed in crammed classrooms, they always bring something home."

"Have a brandy and beer while you're here—that ought to fix you up."

"Just the second half of that—the draft," and I pour and give him it, he says "How much?" I say "First's on me if you don't mind, especially when you didn't take the brandy," and he says "No way, leastwise today," and gives me a dollar, I give him change and he puts a quarter tip on the bar.

"I wasn't trying to manipulate you or anything," I say going downstairs with him. "Not for a few cents—that isn't what I was trying to do. Anybody, my feeling goes, even the mayor, is also a potential customer if he lives or works around here or nearby, so the first or second one free is my standard policy."

"It's okay. Don't get alarmed if you are. But I live upstate and go by the rule to get for nothing you got to give for nothing, and so on on my job, so now we're all straight."

I show him the trash bags and tell him why they're there.

"Hiring a carter's your problem, ours is your clientele's health." He writes a violation. "I'm sorry, you think I like doing this? But get all these bags out by this time tomorrow or we'll have to temporarily revoke your health permit which will mean you'll have to close down till the violation's corrected and permit's returned."

"At least let me keep open the bar part."

"Beer's food and you've got olives on the bar and stuff. No, Department regulations are the entire place I'm afraid, so nothing more for me to say."

I don't offer him anything else—not money, which I'm almost tempted to just to relieve from me some of the strain. Or whatever he might like: though I never did it before or my father if he was telling the truth. I know from other bartenders where some inspectors have taken women as payment or TV's or sports tickets or washers for their wives or in the old days suits for themselves and radios. But I can see by his face and personality where it would only get me in much worse.

That evening while drinking with a customer at the bar I tell him my dilemma from almost the beginning and say "I'm at a loss now to know what to do. You used to have a store, Red. What way in the same spot would you get rid of your trash without having the same bags pile up on you with twice as many others the next day?"

"Take them to the garbage pier."

"What garbage pier where?"

"Uptown along the river on the West Side where they unload all the city's garbage into barges and tug them out to the ocean to dump. You want a van, say the word. A friend for a small fee for him and me. You have to do the driving, I'll only help you pile them in, as I don't want to get too involved in this if those shits who are screwing you are as serious as you say."

I call Sanitation and learn it's okay to unload my trash at the pier after two a.m. when there'll be no city garbage trucks to interfere with. I give Red the money. He comes by around one with the van and we fill it up with bags. He says "I wish I could help you with the second load but have to get some sleep."

"Next round I can probably do myself though it'll probably kill me."

"Make sure you get the van back to my friend before you croak or he'll kill me. While it's still out you, me and the bar are on loan."

I drive to the Sanitation dock, enter the pier through a gate onto this old covered wooden structure like an old-fashioned covered bridge upstate but much longer and which has at the end of it floating in the river a huge barge. I back up and drop my bags in it one by one. All kinds of things are already in the barge and as trash some I've never seen before. A hammock that looks brand new. If I had any use for one or knew anybody who did and felt it'd be safe to climb in to get it, I would. A set of golf clubs, half a big tree, what seems like a good restaurant freezer, shrubs that have green flowers on them so they must've been growing indoors, a bunch of small men's hats the same size it seems and in what look like perfect blocked condition and shape and some still fitted bottomside up in lidless hat boxes. Rats are in the barge also and mice or maybe they're baby rats, these mice, a special river barge kind, not like what I've seen in my bar cellar from time to time. And various animal carcasses. I almost think a dead human hand sticking up, its fingers outstretched, with the rest of the body underneath covered by garbage. Next time I drop a bag in I think it's definitely a human hand with blood on it even and on the forearm puncture marks and around the wrist a patient's identification bracelet. I drive to the man at the gate who seems to be in charge here. He says "It's probably your imagination or part of a store manikin or something," and I say "No, it really looks real, come and see."

"It's happened before, I won't say it hasn't. One time I found five whole baby bodies in it and not fetuses, all tied together and gagged and smothered, worse thing anyone's ever seen here. It made the papers."

"I think I remember hearing of it."

"You'd have had to. None were traceable, case went unsolved, all sorts of speculation, no crime could have been viler unless there were more bodies of them. Let's take a look if you insist."

We get in a two-seater electric cart and when we're halfway there he stops and says "Oh yeah, now I recall, sorry for wasting your time, because I was to expect them. A small truckload of cadavers from a medical school, or parts of what's left of them, arms and legs and things, no heads, that's not allowed to be scrapped the law says. I think next time they should consign them to a common pauper's grave, but I suppose they think what use would a nameless tomb be to anyone and also the expense and who'd keep it up over the years?''

"In the special field they have, the city.''

"Then it's you and me, Jack, you and me and every taxpayer, which comes from our billfolds. Better here.''

"I don't mind paying for it when it's just a few cents per taxpayer, especially when I now know they're ending up here and then the ocean.''

"They don't float, they sink, nothing to bother your beach house about unless they have an unusual bloated condition. And it's good for the water and earth and so eventually us. Helps replenish the minerals in them exactly like everything we excrete.''

"I still think it's worth a check to see if that hand's not connected to somebody murdered.''

"No, I know what it is, was forewarned,'' and he drives to his wooden shack by the gate, I get out and drive to the barge and drop some more bags in it, trying to cover the hand which I can't stand seeing anymore. One of my bags finally knocks it over and the next one sinks it.

A truck pulls up. Private carter, not from one of the companies I know of. Man jumps out of the cab, dump part of the truck rises to about forty-five degrees up and the back flap flips open, something like a coal chute drops out and the garbage starts sliding down it into the barge.

"What are you doing here?'' the man says. With a long iron hook he's dislodging some garbage stuck at the sides of the raised rear.

"My bags. I'm all done but this one.''

"You private or public?''

"I own a bar if that's what you mean.''

"That's where your bags come from?''

"No, from home.''

"What's in it then?" and he slashes the bag I'm holding with his hook.

"All right," when the bottles drop out, "they're from my bar, what of it?"

"What of it is what are you trying to do, put us out of work? Get off the dock with your garbage and don't come back."

"Hey look, don't talk to me like that. I've had more than enough crap from you private garbage guys."

He puts the hook up to my face. "Smell this. Smell good? Smell like dogwood? Your face and van's going to smell like this when I push both you and it into the barge after splitting your nose and tires. Because store people start depositing their garbage here to save on the private costs and not one of us truckers will have a job. Foy?"

Driver gets out of the cab. Big guy also. Both bigger and much younger than me and I'm big. Truck's rear is still in midair but only some dark liquid's dribbling down the chute. Nobody else is around. Electric cart's parked the length away of three city blocks and man's probably in the shack.

"I wish you fellows would understand me but it seems—"

"That's right," Foy says.

"That's what I said. And you can see," bending over, "by my head that I'm not here for trouble and have really had plenty of it, so excuse me," and I go back to the van holding the slashed bag together so nothing will spill out and drive off the pier, honk my horn thanks to the shack, leave the bag in front of a store where there's garbage and drive back to the bar.

I fill the van with the remaining bags and get very tired doing this and my headache comes back bad. I think I feel blood running down my neck and in the dark outside taste it and it's sweat. I haven't really cried for I don't know how many years when all of a sudden there it is. What's making me so sad? and I answer to myself it's probably my head that hurts worse than it has in days that's causing some chain reaction to the tear ducts or whatever they are that start the crying process off and that squeezing feeling inside my neck and chest. But that's not it. I know what it is. It's my weariness and frustration with just about everything concerned with this trash thing from the beginning and my near future prospects in the bar combined. Is that it? That's it or close as I can get. Then go inside, not out here, someone might pass, and let it out for once and maybe you'll feel better and I go in the bar, lock the door, pull down the shades, try and cry but can't now and pour a double, shoot it down, another and yell "Cocksuckers, motherfuckers, I hate all you guys, every last bastard one," and throw the empty glass against the wall and almost collapse from the effort and maybe from my yelling as well and rest a bit more and drink just a single and put an icepack to the hurt part of my head and get back in the van and drive across the bridge singing from all the liquor I drank and actually feeling happy till I thought of it and drop off a bag here and there in that borough and drive to the borough next to it and drop off a few more. When I'm walking back to the van with almost all the bags gone a police car pulls up alongside of me and its top lights blink on and start spinning.

"Mind holding there a second?" the driver says when I open the van door.

"Oh sure, anything, what else could be new?" and I stick a few mints in my mouth.

"You know what you've done is against the law," other officer says, both getting out of the car.

"Wait a second, what is, what've I done?—crying? trying?" and think stop, shut up, you're high, wise up, that's what your mints were for.

"Why you acting stupid? Leaving your garbage around here like you've been doing."

"Was not. I was collecting it. Only opening these bags and cans to see if anything of value's inside. This is a fancy area. People around here got money up their ass to throw out fantastic trash that I sell as junk and antiques to antique and junkstores, whichever which."

"We've been following you. And you smell from alcohol.

Turn around. Put your hands on the van and spead your legs wide.''

I do. "All right," when I'm being patted up and down. "I had some. I won't lie. But I'm not drunk. You want to frisk my trash bags also, go ahead. Black one's mine. Also the one on the extreme left, so be my guests. But none of the others. Never dropped off more than two to each stop and usually one.'' They're through. I turn around. "Because I'm not greedy. Not a collector too. Name's Shaney Fleet. I'm a barowner, cheap joint. Here's my address and name,'' and show them my driver's license and election registration card, only two identifications. "So it's all just bar and grill trash I was dumping because I can't get rid of it any other way. If you knew how far I've come to dump it, you'd laugh.''

"Let's see this 'just bar trash,''' and he opens a pocketknife.

"Don't. I'll only have to carry it back slashed and spilling to the van, which I rented and have to keep clean. I'll do it." I unknot the two bags I left out here and three in the van and they look inside all of them.

"What's wrong?" the driver says. "Business so bad you can't afford a regular pickup?''

"No company will take mine. It's a long story.''

"By law one of them has to. You're either not asking the right firm in the right way or they're in their rights to refuse you because you don't want to pay today's inflated prices.''

"See this head?" I take off my cap. "That's further on. Listen from the beginning and maybe you can advise me. Two men came in my bar a long time ago. Month? Could it be three? I forget. But Turner and Pete. Oh, very sweet guys these two, your mothers would've loved them and I bet in several names they have records a leg long, and they said they represented—'' but he cuts me off and says "We'd be interested if it was in our precinct. Tell whoever the cops are in yours.''

"Everytime I yell for the police these days they won't believe me.''

"Cry fire, not police. That's what I tell my wife. Okay, different situation, but maybe there's something you can learn from it, because she's in alone, couple punks raping her God forbid, neighbors will stay behind their doors if she shouts 'Someone get the police.' So cry fire I tell her and they'll all run out and bat down her door with their heads if they have to to stop the fire from spreading to theirs." He writes up a ticket for illegally dumping refuse on the street while the other calls in the van's license number and description and my name and bar address in case I'm tagged around here again.

"Now get your garbage and drop it in some other precinct, not ours."

I tie up the bags and carry them to the van. I could probably get rid of them in another borough or by the river but I don't want to chance getting caught by the police who might call in and link me with the last ticket and pull me and the van in, making the van owner angry and maybe my staying overnight in jail again and whatever that might bring on. I drive back to the bar, think what would be worse: bags downstairs or on the street? and I carry them downstairs. Only five of them and if the health inspector asks why they weren't dumped with the rest I'll say "Those are today's."

I drive to the motel parking space I'm supposed to leave the van at, honk two dots and a dash to signal the loaner his car's back and cab to my hotel.

"You worked much later than usual," the nightclerk says. "All recovered?"

"Almost. Goodnight."

"You have messages. Not that I'm a snoop, but I don't understand them. Gruff but educated man phoned them in practically an hour apart to the second you'll see dutifully marked on the time slot."

I read them. "Boiling hot out today isn't it?" the first says. "Boiling hot out tonight isn't it?" the second says.

"Firstly," he says, "they were phoned in at nine and ten at night so what's with the 'today' and 'tonight' distinction? Okay. Your privilege not to answer and minor point. Secondly, your caller can't be talking about the weather of course, because I froze my rear off getting here.''

"It is cold. When I was outside I wasn't even thinking of it but it must be near zero.''

"Three above? Your room will be freezing now and by five there'll be icicles inside. Want to borrow an electric blanket? Small charge.''

"I'm afraid of fires in those things. I'll cover the covers with my coat.''

"Then if you weren't a barowner I'd say 'Like a bottle sent up?' ''

"I would. Forgot mine and I've run out. Scotch, oldest and best you got. I feel I deserve it.''

"Like a little lady also? She lives here but doesn't work out of the hotel and told me for my special friends she's on call anytime.''

"No. It's been so long I forgot.''

"Don't worry what she thinks. And baby-cute, dancer's boobs, and to even men who are eighty and have no chance in the world of reaching it she never makes them feel like fools.''

"Just the scotch.''

"Give me ten minutes to age it.''

Knocks on my door while I'm under a cold shower because there's no hot and I'm pig-filthy and reek. I yell "Hold it," get in a bathrobe and then a coat and go to the door, pay him and give a tip. "Who minds the store while you're delivering?''

"That mean you want to chat and offering me a drink?''

"Sure.''

"I bolt the lobby door. —Pour just a trickle more. Switchboard rings or guests want to come in and their frozen fingers are falling off, let them—I have to turn an extra bill over my salary or my family and I can't survive. When people complain I say 'Diseased bladder.' ''

"So you're married.''

"Oh yes, it's the best thing. Cheers," and we click glasses and drink.

"When do you see your wife, and children?"

"Children sure. Why do without? Wife when I come home and snuggle into her an hour before she has to roust the house and kids and on my one night off. That's time enough."

"I ought to get married. Never bothered me till now and I haven't spoken of it much before, but I'm damn lonely and for some probably logical reason getting lonelier every day."

"Marriage covers lots of rough spots. Not that I want to force you into it, Mr. Fleet—Shaney may I call you now? And facetiously force you into it of course. Anyway, my petty enterprising is piss poor in this dive, since how many fine scotch tipplers and horny guys you think I've got? I only stay here because this hotel is still keeping barely alive, and locatable nightclerk jobs in safe neighborhoods are short. But if you're seriously interested in getting connected, then once you give up your bandage and blackeye disguise and grow in the shaven scalp hair, there's another little lady here, this one maybe big once but now stooped through age and not so shapely or cute, who's quite rich and only tolerating substandard housing because she abhors hostel snobbery as she says. She lives on the sixth and is looking for a much younger man than she for companionship and to run errands and eventually keep and every so often if the desire moves her, a little physical diddling, and if it works out for both of them, inheritance and wedlock. We could pretend you're ten years younger than you are. For a small part of whatever she contributes to you, I could smooth through the introductions and claim you're Casanova come back."

"No, with me it's got to be to fall-in-love. Must seem silly at my age and it's another idea I haven't thought about for years, but I haven't felt strongly for someone since high school."

"This is the one I'd fall for if given half a second chance. Though my wife's all right. Works hard, great mom, lays out for me what I need and carries me through streaks of unemployment and debauchery, so I've no gripes. But think it over. And you must be freezing and I have to leave. Sure you don't want the younger one? She can be rung up till past four and then she dreams till noon.''

"No thanks.''

''Then one quick one more. Higher...higher...lower the wrist some—there, and I'll take the glass with me and send it back tomorrow smelling of soap.''

''By the way, if you were interested in a parttime or changing jobs to one with I think better hours and free food and drinks at the end of the day and perhaps more pay—''

''Oh, I don't want to get tangled in what you're presently involved with, kind as you are to ask. Just from those eerie phone voices and your broken skull, it eventually seems fatal.''

I drink some more. Probably just the unusual amount of booze that's making me feel like having sex and I think what the hell, got a few dollars in my pocket and it's been a long time, even though I know it's not right and I could get a disease, but what the hell, tired of doing it to myself when I've the energy to and it's been a long long time and there's always antibiotics if they still work and I call the nightclerk and say ''I don't like asking this, but how much for the younger woman?''

''Sure you don't and don't worry: she's in your means. I'll have her rap on your door and you can catch me next loop around.If you want more from her the price rises by halves for each added service and a cut higher than that if what you want is bizarre, but nobody has enough cash for her to get kicked or slapped.''

''I only want the natural way once.''

''Twenty then.''

''Seems more than fair.''

She taps. I don't want to answer, hold my breath. She taps. I get an erection, let her in, am nervous, in my street clothes, offer her a drink. She's young and okay-looking and small and already taking her sweater off with nothing on underneath, and underneath has a couple of long stomach scars and stitch marks and pregnant belly I think and almost flat breasts, so I guess that's what a dancer's are, though I wouldn't bet.

She says "No thanks, maybe just a glass of water if you wouldn't mind. Let the tap run as the water here straight out of the faucet tastes like car oil, you find the same with yours?" Now naked, sitting on the bed, legs a little spread, squeezing something on her thigh. "Yes I'm pregnant if that's what you're gaping at and seems to be disturbing you. If it does I can go, no trouble, and you don't have to pay me a thing. You want me to? Good. Take off your clothes, you're making me feel like I undressed on the street and it's not just the cold. Any other night I'd give you plenty more time if you wanted it, the whole foreplay, but can we start soon?—I'm pooped. But my water first. And wash your penis clean while you're in there and then come and get on top and stick it right in—I'm ready. I might look frail but can handle three times my own weight."

I wash, give her the glass of water and sit next to her on the bed.

"Don't worry about the fetus either if that's what's bothering you now—it'll be dead in a few days anyway. Not a legal clinic, I'm too far gone for them, but a good butcher. But let's forget all that now—get in here. Not around my knees but between them—that's right, that's nice, just the way you're moving."

Later she says "Truthfully I should be paid time and a half for what it took you, but you're probably just a bit intoxicated and tired. At least your body was clean and not so fat and you were a gentleman and didn't fake like a lot of men do that it wasn't great and you didn't squirt, just so you can get, after a long wait, your second as a freebie. Night-night, sweetheart. Beginning Wednesday I'll be recuperating for a few days from the operation. After or before that if you want me again, help me skip the fee to the nightclerk. Just go outside and from the booth across the street dial the hotel direct. My name's Helena, and maybe you can disguise your voice a bit when you ask him for it, and I'm in 807."

After she leaves I scrub my genitals, just to be on the safe side, and have a drink and think I should get married. Someone to talk and get warm to and occasionally do it with but free from possible disease. And maybe to help around the bar like my mother with my father did, cooking big dishes at home for it and some table and counter serving at lunch where we could earn a little extra through her tips. But I don't want to do it again, though it felt good, with a hooker. Not enough of that feeling of blamelessness and routine, so too much like doing it with my own kid or close niece.

Next day a few hours earlier than he said he would the health inspector comes in, shakes the sleet off his hat and asks to be taken to the basement. I pick up the bar slats, open the floor hatch and we go downstairs.

"I do have a couple of bags here from today, but all of yesterday's I got rid of."

"That's good. Makes my job easier." He takes a penlight out of his coat pocket and shines it on the bags. The light's violet instead of white. He turns each of the bags over with the penlight always on them, though the ceiling bulb seems bright enough to see whatever he's interested in.

"So. Going to close me for a few recent bags?"

"Hey, let's cut out all the horseshit before we sink in it. Come here," and he points to where the beam's aimed at. There's a little X on the bag and some scribbling beneath it. "That's my mark and initials and yesterday's time and day. I wrote it with an ink you can only read with this light. I didn't X all your bags, though two of these have it on them."

"Maybe you marked them just now, because I'm telling you all the bags here come just from today."

"Did you see me just mark them?"

"If I didn't see you yesterday, how could I today?"

"Yesterday you left me alone for a few moments. Anyway, the city will know it's yesterday's because I'm taking this one with me. You'll let me, of course."

"What could I do to stop you?"

"You could not block my way for one thing."

"Oh, I thought something else."

"Huh?"

"Nothing. I'm confused and disturbed. Why shouldn't I be? You think I've another living going? A rich father? Sure I do, but what I thought you meant— Not bribery for sure. I hope that's not what you thought. But you know: a hot coffee or cocoa was what I was offering you because of the cold, that's all. Look, I apologize, forget everything I said, but you finally want the truth of the matter?"

"You mean what you just said hasn't been? No no, I'm kidding, go on."

"The truth is I dumped and this is the honest truth, dumped all of yesterday's garbage from yesterday's bags into cardboard boxes and shopping bags and drove them to the Sanitation pier to dump. Call the guard at the gate shack there if the same one's working late tonight and he'll tell you he saw me around two: blue van and that he also gave me a ride in his electric cart when I thought I saw a dead human hand that was only a cadaver's in their barge and so didn't count. But the plastic bags from yesterday I reused today, because buying them even by the ton runs into more money than my poor business can afford. But I had a feeling before you wouldn't believe me, so I told you the hoax story of these bags being fresh, which the garbage still is, from today."

"Then you have yesterday's bags here, which as far as the Health Department's concerned is yesterday's garbage, since the dirty bags should have been dumped too."

"What I say you wouldn't believe me."

"Who doesn't? And please fight it if you like. That's what our Administrative Tribunal's for. Most of us inspectors love it when the less reprehensible stores like yours win, as we don't see any gain for the city when you go out of business and possibly on welfare. At a hearing this week you can show why you failed to abide by the Health Code. If the tribunal judges against you, you'll be fined. If it also decides, which is usually the case, that you're entitled to a third inspection and at that inspection you've corrected your violations and can show proof of new arrangements where they won't be repeated, your health permit will be restored.''

"How can I show the inspector I've corrected and won't repeat my violations if I'm not being allowed to correct and not repeat by this company of hoods?"

"Coercion's a civil court matter, not Health's. Ours is simply to see that all the food stores and restaurants meet the Health Code."

"But I won't be able to prove anything to any court that I'm being threatened or other people are. I've no evidence of it and nobody who knows about it will be brave or dumb enough to testify."

"All I'm saying is if you can prove to a civil court judge that you have been intimidated, then the court will probably make this company pay your fines, give you loss-of-business restitution and also issue an injunction against them to stop molesting you. Then you'll be able to hire another carter for your garbage which will mean you'll have corrected your violations and made arrangements not to repeat them. As of this moment though I have to ask you to tell your customers upstairs to go and for you to lock up and not enter the bar again for customers till we restore your health permit. Do and the tribunal might rule that you lose your health permit for good. If you don't close voluntarily now I'll call a cop and city carpenter and have a hasp and padlock put on your door and remove yours. Touch our lock and you'll be arrested and probably prohibited from handling liquor or food anywhere in the state again in a commercial way."

"Close me. Don't know from where but I'll come up with something to open again."

"That's the only way to do it, Mr. Fleet—peacefully and optimistically."

We go upstairs, he carrying my garbage bag. He's a weak little guy or looks it and I say "Can I help you with that, no evil influence intended," and he says no. I tell the one customer to pay up and go. As he's leaving the bar I say "Wait, Walt—

106

here's your three bucks back. If you're going to be my last customer then I want it to be like my father did, which was to buy everybody at the bar a last round before he turned the place over to me with this immediate huge deficit. Of course he had them three deep that night and his leaving was like a going-off-to-war celebration, when I just have you two here. You want one, sir?" I say to the inspector. "Even just that coffee or cocoa?"

"Can't. I'm not even permitted to purchase a matchbook in any establishment I'm examining." He takes my health permit off the wall, has me sign a release that he took it and puts the permit and release in his briefcase.

"I'll be twenty minutes."

I tear down the bar, wipe it clean, shut the lights, lock up and he asks for and I give him the keys. I sign another release for them and he tapes a sign on the door: "Premises Temporarily Closed by Order of Dept. of Health."

"Everyone who reads that will think I've roaches and rats galore in there and never come back to eat."

"Have them phone me and I'll guarantee you've one of the cleanest bars in town."

"Want to know something? Maybe I'm cutting my throat by this but I want to say it anyway as a sign of my sincerity. I've seen occasional rats and mice in my cellar and of course roaches and trapped or poisoned them or chased them out and sealed up their escape holes. And a couple of times in recent years here an animal or two I've never seen before. I don't even know where this thing comes from and never saw a picture of it in any encyclopedia or animal book when I went to look or heard or read of it talked about. They've long slithering flat tails and big round ears and little kids' baby teeth and faces like platypuses these nonrats, though they're no larger than our average-sized mice. Once or twice I swear I saw them and when I did they got scareder than I was and darted into the dark together and disappeared, not to be seen by me for another two years. They must come from the sewers through holes or pipes in my wall from yesteryear that are behind things that I think are for something else or never knew were there.''

''Several other bar places around town have told me about them. They're little and light brown, right? and—''

'' 'Little' I said and that shade of color, yes.''

''And seem to thrive on underground dampness and coolness and garbage and the seepage from kegs of ale and beer. They apparently only travel in twos and are probably of opposite sexes our resident pest specialist says, since one's always a lot furrier than the other and less the aggressor, but which sex that one is she doesn't know. Nobody's been bitten or even touched one yet though they say they have been sissed and spit at. You'd think, knowing the personality and armory you bartenders got, that in the fifteen years since they were first sighted, one of these cellar creatures would have been caught or shot or with a beer bottle or bat clubbed to unconsciousness or found one time down there after they had died a natural death. Since they've so far remained relatively timid and for all we know might be the same two going from bar to bar through their own subterranean paths, we kept it on the q.t. to the news so as not to alarm and frighten off the entire bar population and your clientele. But we would appreciate and are even offering a small reward and citation to the first bar worker who captures one alive and a small reward without the citation for one dead in almost any recognizable form, not that we're encouraging anyone to endanger his life doing it.''

''So I learned I wasn't crazy all along about these animals, which always till now kept me from telling anyone.''

We shake hands in front of the bar and he wishes me well and I walk in the falling snow to my hotel. Dayclerk's on duty behind the desk and he says ''Never seen you here this early. What's wrong, you sick?''

''Just very upset. If my luck gets any worse—well, I don't know, I haven't all day stepped in dogshit yet. Any messages?''

Letter from the cemetery my family's at, forwarded from my old address and requesting a teller's check for the gravesite's annual maintenance. "This is our final reminder. Snow covers a multitude of untidinesses but does melt. If you cannot settle this debt by next week we will distressingly be compelled to let the ground of your deceased loved ones overgrow."

Other another bill from my previous landlord demanding I pay all of last month's rent, even though I was burned out three days into it. Since, to get her off my back, I already sent her half a month's rent and figure because she's such a shrewdie she'll collect fire insurance on my apartment fire worth five times what it'll cost her to rebuild and then get twice the monthly rent I paid, I tear the bill up and drop it in the cigarette butt can by the elevator.

"Please for godsakes don't throw your trash in there," the dayclerk says. "That's for tobacco objects only, which could ignite your letters and end up burning down the hotel."

I pick the paper scraps out, shake the sand off and put them in my pocket. Helena comes out of the elevator as I'm about to go in it and I tip my hat at her. She acts like she doesn't know me and I hold the elevator button at L and say "Shaney, tenant in the hotel here, friend of the nightclerk Eric, how you doing?"

"Oh yeah or at least I think so. This morning, am I wrong? I was so freaking sleepy and didn't have in my lens. Fine thanks," and stands there staring at me and I say "Well, isn't fair keeping other people upstairs from using the elevator, so I'll be seeing you," and she pinches my sleeve and says "Want company? I could take an hour's detour and you were terrific last time, despite what I might have said in my sleepiness—you really got me going," and I say "Not today thanks though thanks for asking, I mean that, and you know I didn't do anything of the kind to you," and go in the elevator and press my button.

"Don't depreciate yourself," she says as the door closes, "or you'll never get anywheres good."

There's a lilac smell she left that I like and I almost feel like riding up and down another time to keep sniffing it. Reminds me of me on her, just faint traces of her body especially around the armpits and breasts, though mixed with my liquor and after awhile her sweat. And also of my grandmother when I was a boy, not only the toilet water she always wore but the bunches of lilacs she vased in one vase on their bar's free food counter every spring and made me trolley from home at least once a year then to smell them. "Stick your big nose in there, kiddy," she'd say. She and my grandfather are also at that gravesite.

In my room for almost nothing better to do I take the bandage off even if I've a week to and stick it in the wastepail. Maybe the wound will heal faster in just plain air but what the hell do I know? In the mirror I've a long raw ditch in my head and the stitches have almost disappeared. Metal plate inside my skull I'm afraid to touch I can't even look where. Otherwise I'm quite a mess. Bags under my eyes, lost weight in the neck and face, skin paler, hair greyer, right side of my head again hurts, eyeballs bloodshot when I never noticed them anything but all white before, even my teeth ache. So my bar's locked up. All right, forget it for now. If anything, till you get yourself more in control, just try and joke about it, and ten seconds later: piss, shit! How'll I make my way when I haven't got hardly a pot saved to lick from and have to soon pay the bar rent and other bills and this hotel in a few days? and I slam the medicine chest door till the water glass falls off the toothbrush holder underneath and bounces around in the sink while I try to catch it before it breaks.

I drink a stiff drink and another and slap the mattress with my fists and shout "Christ, sons of bitches," and then think easy there, getting nowhere by this, they could knock down the door and lock you up for being a sicko for all you know and I lie on the bed and think what to do to get my permit back and stop from losing my bar for good and right away drop off for an hour when I was trying my hardest not to.

I dream about being naked in bed with Helena though here she has specks for breasts and a much larger rear but is her same age and I'm only a year older than her and she comments on my "delicious sunbit skin." She's supposed to be my sister, a telegram she hands me says, who in truth died of a doctor's mishap at home when she was eleven and me twelve and is also at that gravesite. And just when I'm about to shoot in her with more body thrills and force and noise than I had in real life this morning and maybe ever and Helena screaming my ears out too, I awake from the sound of a Sanitation snowplow grating against the pavement.

I pace around the room and can't think of a thing to do about how to reopen the bar and get my trash picked up on a regular basis. Tribunal? What do I have for it and another inspector that's new? Lawyer? Just for a talk with one what's to lose? I fish out the business card that lawyer slipped into my wallet at the hospital ward, call her and say "Janie Pershcolt? Shaney Fleet here, remember me?" and she says "Sure, how are you, what's up?" and I tell her what's happened till now to me since I last saw her, and when she asks, refresh her memory a little about what went on before.

"You know, for a moment I couldn't place you apart from the rest of my prison charges but now I do. How's your gash? You really got stabbed bad."

"Hit with a pipe. Bandage came off today."

"Knife or pipe, it's cause for celebration, right? because it means the doctors think you're getting well, so I'm glad."

"I took the bandage off myself, so I don't know if it was the best thing."

"Don't worry, you look better with it off, right? And when you look better your spirits soar, which always improves the healing process, so coming up right behind it should be your complete cure. Okay, what I can do for you straight off the skin of my head is the following. Present the civil court a petition of redress in your name exerting upon them in no uncertain terms the pressing need if not fullfledged professional necessity on your part to, nah, that won't do. Your predicament's more complex. Give me a day to filter through it. But it by all means seems, and this is from the heart, not the legalese brain, that every human being conducting a legitimate business in the city ought to have the indivisible right to get his commercial trash collected just as every private carter ought to have the same right to refuse to handle a customer if it's not because of race, religion, sex and the rest of those reasons. But let me quote my rates so we later don't have to resort to blows over it because we didn't know such and such was the price, right? For the brief I'll have to draw up in your behalf in the next few days and which should rescind your fines and violations, impose a restraining order on Stovin's and force one of the other carters to accept you as a client, it'll be eight hundred dollars plus whatever ancillary expenses are required for cabs and calls and so forth, agreed?''

''I don't have that kind of money.''

''You own a bar, don't you, so you must do well.''

''It's a small inexpensive joint for too much rent and with all the companies who service me raising their prices from month to month. It barely stays afloat.''

''Then sell it, because you can't win without a lawyer. With the rest of the money from your bar's sale and possibly compensatory penalties you'll get from Stovin's, you can open another place.''

''I couldn't get much for the bar. Maybe a little something for a few of the older fixtures. But nothing enough for opening a new bar and zero from anyone for taking over the bar's name and lease.''

''What kind of ready money do you have then?''

''A hundred, fifty, like that but at the most.''

''To get even the brief typed without pages of smudge marks and wine stains and a couple of court copies made will cost me more than that.''

''Then how about one of those free voluntary whatever-they-are lawyer organizations for people like me who can't afford high fees?''

''Mine's not high, it's low. But because it's the slow season and with my own onslaught of bills to pay, I could reduce it for you by two hundred or so.''

"I still can't, so what about that Legal Aid group?"

"I hope your joint earned you a poverty level income or less last year and the state declared you an indigent, because if not, Legal Aid can't touch you."

"I at least got above poverty, thank God."

"Was what you earned the same amount you reported?"

"Every penny I made I reported and paid all the taxes on too."

"No wonder you're in so steep. I don't know what to say, baby. You haven't the money, then you can't engage me and for sure no other lawyer and you're now wasting what might be left of your hard-earned income on what I charge for professional advice over the phone. That costs twenty dollars per quarter of an hour, seventy-five for the full. If I handled your case that charge would be appliable to the big fee. Since we only spoke fourteen minutes, my timer says, plus my chitchat now about what I cost over the phone and so forth, which I don't charge for but is time-consuming. I'll make it a flat seventeen just for you. Mail it to my business card address."

"What I phoned for wasn't so much advice but an estimate."

"Fifteen then, but that's rock bottom."

"Still, it doesn't seem fair."

"You send me that fifteen, chiseler, or I'll haul you into Small Claims and get you for what you owe me plus what my rates are to take two hours away from work and cab fare back and forth," and hangs up.

I call back and say "Listen, Mrs. or Miss Pershcolt, don't forget how you first got me. I'll tell the judge that by law you're not supposed to take me on as a private client when I was originally assigned to you as a public."

"You win, you mooch, but I hope those Stovin creeps and all the city department slobs wind up with your shirt, socks and jockeyshorts and whatever you got underneath and in the middle of a major street."

"Thanks, *lady*."

"Oh, you going to be so asinine to give me an argument about that too?"

"No, I don't know what asinine is, but go on, get out of my life—die why don't you please, you SOB," I scream and she's laughing and I hang up.

I think give it up, sell out, let it go for peanuts if that's the only way to get rid of it, walk away from it even if that's what it has to come down to, start another bar in some other city or a different business in this one or work for a barowner or chain or just give yourself the time to do whatever you want to do with the money you might end up making from the bar's sale. But those aren't constructive thoughts how to deal with the two main problems: what to do about reopening the bar and carting away its garbage, so think some more.

Maybe if I don't think about it and do something else for the next few hours or entire day, something will come to my head like a bomb going off. But what do I know from anything to do but work, eat, sleep and now drink? I pour another scotch and think forget that too: you'll be blind by the night and a lush by morning or getting to be with maybe never another constructive thought about anything again but taking another drink, which isn't.

I pour the scotch back in the bottle, lick my fingers where it dripped, put my rubbers and coat on and go to a movie house around the block just to do something but thinking about drinking and the garbage and bar.

Nobody stands so I squeeze along my aisle, brush an opened box of candy off my seat, sit down, my foot accidentally kicking an empty beer or soda can which rolls a few rows to the front before stopping I suppose against a seat leg or someone's shoe. But I leave in an hour. After twenty or more years of not seeing a picture except on the bar's TV, and that just snatches of but I don't think ever a whole one straight through, it seems I've lost all interest in them or just can't get in the mood and also every seat I tried was too uncomfortable with springs popping or padding sticking out and the theater seemed infested besides.

I buy a book off the paperback rack at the drugstore and go to a coffeeshop and read it while having a sandwich and milkshake. It's a novel about an old plantation family years ago. Maybe it's a good story and the writing's surely all right and scenes and people true to life or at least what I know from those days, but the book or maybe just reading them or particularly at this time just isn't for me. I give the book to the counterman along with my tip and money for the check and he says "Don't bother, I can hardly rest long enough to breathe."

"Give it to a customer and he'll appreciate it and maybe give you a bigger tip."

"All right, I'll give it to a customer. Hey mac," he says to me, "like to read a terrific spicy new pocketbook for free?" and we laugh and I lay down an extra quarter to my tip and take the book and drop it in a trashcan on the street. Now that's the type of guy I should've got to work for me when I had the chance: tough but good sense of humor and smart and he looks honest and reliable, though who can tell till you really see?

I'd like to go to the park just to walk and in the quiet think, but it's freezing and getting dark and I'm a little afraid to after what I've heard and read in the news what happens in there.

I go back to the hotel and watch TV in the lounge. The people there are so noisy and such a bunch of sad old rummies who make me feel sad that I rent my own set, carry it up, turn it on, off, in ten minutes I can tell that all late afternoon television, in the lounge or anywheres, is just too dumb and phony for me. But what does a person do when he has nothing to do and plenty of time to do it in? I lie on the bed and play with myself just to again do something and maybe get off a bit of tension and see the cemetery letter on the dresser while I'm doing this and think that I still haven't sent the check for the gravesite's maintenance yet. And then that I haven't been out there for years because I couldn't find the time to and that might be a good spot to forget all my bar problems and such till I suddenly in the quiet there solve them.

I call the cemetery and get directions because I forgot them after all these years. "It's late," person I speak to says, "but you can make it if you catch the next train and grab a cab at the station."

I put on my warmest clothes and boots and catch that train. It doesn't move for a half-hour after departure time and then goes unusually slow for even a suburban train, getting to the station an hour later than it was expected and a few minutes before the cemetery's supposed to close.

I get a cab at the station and the driver starts taking me a different way. "Where you going?" I say. "I remember the ride and unless all the roads have changed since or they've moved the cemetery, then at that light back there you should've made a left instead of a right, because I know it's not down this drive."

"You said Saint Athemus, correct? So this is the quickest most direct way there."

"I told you Pearlwood, loud and clear—Pearlwood, so don't give me it you didn't hear."

"I didn't. You claiming I did? I didn't. I distinctly heard you say Athemus. But you don't like the way I drive or a man can't make a simple mistake with you, which mine only might've been but I swear wasn't, then what do you want me to do?"

"To be absolutely fair, deduct a half-dollar off the meter and I'll be satisfied."

"And have it come from my pocket? Because that's what my boss will want. He'll say I was cheating him."

"I'll write a note for you that you weren't."

"He won't take notes. He'll say I could've signed anyone's name to it and he could be right."

"I'll put on it my phone number and address."

"For the fifty cents owed him you think he'll phone you on what could be a dollar call? Just tell me you'll pay the full fare that's on the meter or I'll have to let you off here."

"You leave me out here wherever the hell we are and I'll tear the back of your cab apart."

"Try and I'll lock you in and call Cab Control who'll call the cops."

116

He presses a button on the steering wheel and all the door locks snap down another notch. I try pulling up my lock but can't. There's a steel screen between us and I say through it "Okay okay, no more complaints. Get to Pearlwood fast as you can and I'll pay."

"Now you're talking sense."

He turns the cab around and drives to Pearlwood and stops at the cemetery gate and says through the screen "Eight dollars."

"Meter reads four-fifty."

"I have to ride back and have no customers here because your cemetery's closed. And I don't feel like waiting for you, even if you wanted me to, at the dollar-every-three-minutes time. For one reason, you might leave through one of the side ways if you got in and for another, I know you're not giving a tip. So the eight or I take you back to the station and let you off after you pay the four-fifty plus whatever the new reading is from here to there."

I put a ten in the screen tray and he gives me two dollars change and presses the button that releases the locks. I get out.

"Piece of advice," he says.

"I'll give you."

"No listen, see that phonebooth there? When you call a Meyermeg cab to get back, don't ask for Nate's."

"Bastard," I yell. He waves and drives away. Never should've yelled anything like that in front of here. About death I'm a bit superstitious and make the religious sign with my fingers over my chest and then think that's ridiculous and rub it off and ring the bell on the cemetery gate. Voice on an intercom above the bell says "Cemetery closed for the day."

"Please, I've come a long way."

"Sorry, closed, good day."

"Look, I haven't seen my parents or sister in years and I can get out here just about never."

"Next time come earlier."

"Next time I will, that's a promise, but this time give me a

117

break."

"I shouldn't but could."

"Yes?"

"That's it. I shouldn't but could."

"So what'll it take?"

"What are you saying?"

"I'm saying can we talk straight?"

"Anyone with you?"

"You can't see through that camera thing on top of the gate?"

"It's dark behind you. People can lie in shadows and what I'm seeing you through is a cheap set."

"Nobody's with me."

"Then we can talk, but be circumspect."

"Will a five or ten dollar cash contribution get me in for a half hour?"

"Contribution to the cemetery."

"Cemetery."

"Fifteen minutes total is all I can spare you once we reach your plot. You don't know where it is, I can be of service in another way, as I've this direction book to help."

"It's in one of the rows to the right off a driveway. I can't miss it as it's in a meadow almost by itself."

"Others have gone up all around it."

"Louise and Lester Fleet then. And my sister, with the same last name, and our grandparents, Dondon, in adjacent graves."

"All I need. E-F-Fl-Fleet. Agnes. Lester and spouse. Co-related: Beatrice and Daryl Dondon the third. Row 141, section 7S. Wait for me."

Drives down, gets out of his car, says hello and sticks his mitted hand through the gate. I shake it. "That's fine, pleasure's all mine. But the you-know-what."

"I'm not sure anymore I can."

"Don't try to haggle with me, Fleet. The ten-dollar cemetery donation or I ride back and you won't see me again today."

"Please, let me go over with you what I've gone through to get here and why."

"Not interested."

"Don't be such a hard guy."

"Also no time for talk."

"Then just let me in. I don't want to hand over money and it's cost me enough just to come out. And it's my cemetery. My grandfather also reserved space for me here and my wife and kids if I had them."

"You need cash then? Sell your extra plots. There'll be no end to takers. This is a relatively close space to the city, so you'll get plenty for them—ten times what your grandfather paid."

"I don't want to. I still could get married someday and have a kid or already my wife's. And this is holy ground. At least sacred to me with my family in there, so don't make me have to report you."

"You threatening? I'll deny and backfire on you. I'll say you went crazy when you came late and I wouldn't let you in. I'm old and trusted here. Just as I thought you could be trusted— dragging me down here, you son of, and you didn't act that type over the TV screen—so they'll believe me as they know people in grief have tried everything with us day and night and also the owners never heard my doing anything wrong. Not that I ever have or am doing anything wrong now. A contribution to the nondenominational cemetery chapel I'm trying to collect for them they certainly won't frown upon."

"It's a bribe for yourself you want, no contribution."

"Whose bribe? You pushed me and I refused. God, if I had the legal right or my earlier age and strength I'd force you to pay to the cemetery the car gas down here and my wage consumed and maybe for me my medical bills for the temperature I'll probably get standing here and charges. Courtroom charges I'd be using to sue you for breach of everything and filthy slander," and he gets in the car and drives up the hill.

I shake the gate, ring the bell. Maybe someone else is in the office. Nobody answers. I shake, pound the gate with a stone, stay on the bell, still no one answers. I've had it to here with these bastards, had it and shake a fist at the camera and go right along the fence looking for another entrance, but in my five-minute walk through the shin-high snow there is none. I start climbing the iron bar fence. Screw him, I'll get in my own way, but it's slippery with ice and I slide down. I start climbing another less slippery spot but stop halfway up. It's night so how would I find our gravesite? Piled up snow, maybe the graves and stones grown over as well, even with the good moon I got, probably surrounded as he suggested by a thousand headstones by now when before they were alone, and getting back over might even be tougher.

I look through the fence and think I see their headstones in the distance and start to cry. This would be about where they are, same size and rounded on top, each with an inscription on them about something to do with "rest, peace" and "love." Little obelisk for my sister I can't see to the left of them, but it might be some kind of optical illusion stopping me, or knocked down.

I stay there, forehead against the fence, say my own prayer and let their five faces pass through my head, then walk back to the front gate and yell at the intercom "Hey you—caretaker. Next time you come outside the grounds you're going to get one of these here, but with a brick in it for your evil nose," and I make and throw a snowball at the camera and hit a tree way off and get on my knees to make some more. Brick wasn't a serious threat. And why my making these balls for? Police will be called and I got what I mostly came out here for, didn't I? and that's to never let these thieves get to me where I let up or start to beg and I also saw or think I did my sister and folks and spoke a few words to them and thought.

I go to the phonebooth in front and am about to call the cab company when I hear sirens. I run across the road, feign going right, in the dark go left and hide behind a bush about fifty feet from the gate. Police come, look around, ring the bell and care-taker drives down and points in the opposite direction I ran and they shine their flashlights there and then write on a clipboard and he signs it and they go.

He drives up the hill. I wait a while. Moon's bright, with a kindly round face almost upsidedown, and the caws of some big bird or another jumping from tree to tree I'm under. I'd like to get even with the caretaker in some way but a threat. Like prying apart the intercom and camera and have him explain it to the owners. But that in the long run would end up hurting me more than him in cemetery costs and I guess they're also there to protect the graves. Maybe an anonymous letter about his bribery to the owners, but I drop the idea for now and walk along the drive for about a mile toward the train station till I come to a phonebooth in front of the next cemetery. Meyermeg's number is on the phonebooth wall and I call and tell the dispatcher "Send my old friend Nate to pick me and my wife up at Pearlwood. We were inside visiting too long and didn't know the place had closed."

I see Nate pass me as I walk toward town. In the dark I spit at him and would like to tell him a thing or two, but don't want to get caught by the police through his two-way. Then I see him driving back alone and I'm so cold I want to hail him just for the ride and no words, but he'll know the phone trick before was me so I hold back.

I walk the next few miles to town, in a cafe have a coffee and soup and rub my frozen limbs back to life, call a different cab company and because I don't want to be seen by the police where they might be waiting for me at the train station, I tell the driver to take me to the next town's station further out on the island where I have to meet my oldest son. He does, says "Want me to wait?" and I say "No thanks, my wife's coming by car from the other way," and get the train back to the city and subway to my hotel.

"Phone message for you," the nightclerk says.

"Beautiful grave day," it says.

"Listen," I say. "Anyone calls for me like this or any kind, hang up."

"No can do. It could be the cops, Narcotics, parole officers or the like, just for examples, so city regulations say I have to pass every phone and letter message on to the guest."

"If I gave you a fiver you wouldn't, right?"

"As I had to have told you before: that's how I survive here, not that I ever got a dime for doing that. If there's anything guests want it's their messages."

"Well these for me are just a crock to rattle me, I don't want them anymore, and I'm not giving you a five to do anything again but get me a bottle of scotch if I haven't for some dumb reason thought of getting it myself from my bar or before the stores close. But if you do give me another note like this I'm going to rip it to little bits and throw it all over you and your desk, understand?"

"I got ears."

"Just answer if you understand me."

"That's what I meant about my ears. I hear. They're clean, every day dewaxed. So sure, but what are you getting so testy all of a sudden for? I was only carrying out the law to its littlest letters, but now I know better with you. By the way—"

"No."

"Not scotch but perhaps—"

"I know not scotch and what 'perhaps' and I don't want it."

"But you look cold. And she's got a touch of the flu herself, or had, though nothing bad to pass any bug on to you, so she stayed in bed most of the day and by now should be real toasty. Or maybe you're thinking of getting her direct over the phone and not through me."

"No and goodnight."

"If not Helena then, there's another cute girl in the hotel. Blonde, almost as young, but a lot taller and bosomier and with legs that could wrap around a chaise lounge. If you want—"

Elevator door closes and I ride up and go to my room. I'd like a few drinks to warm me and help me get to sleep but want to be up early tomorrow and without a hangover and extra sharp. So I drink plenty of tap water and exercise, warmups,

122

few situps, running in place, and turn on the TV and immediately start yawning, no doubt mostly from all that road walking before and clumping through cemetery snow.

Next morning I go to the Administrative Tribunal office downtown, show the clerk my summons for a hearing later this week and say "I'd like very much to have it pushed up to today."

"Sorry, we've a full workload as it is. If we pushed you up, everyone would want to be pushed up and then we'd be working way over overtime which we don't get paid an extra cent for, so you can see the impossibility of such a move."

"I'm not interested in everyone. Because do you see everyone who has a hearing with you later this week in the room now?"

"Don't you raise your voice to me."

"Then give me a sensible answer why you can't push me up."

"And don't order me to answer you."

"I'm not ordering, I'm asking. But since you are a civil servant supposedly paid to serve citizens like me and I'm a paying taxpayer—"

"And don't give me that outdated fallacious line of argument either. Because thirty-five percent of the city's labor force are paid public servants in one form or another like also state and federal. And we pay as much if not more taxes than most workers and have to put up with the same city machinery, but unlike all the noncivil workers, most of us get no unemployment insurance if we're laid off."

"You get other compensation."

"Abuse, yes, if you like it."

"You get other things. Continual raises for even the ones who don't deserve them. Free subway rides for policemen and stuff and everyone a good pension plan. But how'd we get into this, and I know you're just doing your job. But it does seem, job or not and which should be part of it I'd think, that if someone in my predicament whether I'm a city worker or not makes a reasonable demand from one, then that demand ought to be thought on if not granted if it's not too unreasonable to grant to, which mine isn't. Because you have to get cancellations all the time for your hearings, don't you?''

"If you mean your taking over one of those cancellations, yes, we get several daily, but we take them into consideration when we speak about our full workload each day. It's analogous to the airlines who intentionally, with the consent of the agency regulating them, overbook their flights by fifteen percent because they know a quarter to more reservations and even confirmed tickets will at the last minute—''

I see a well-dressed woman in a suit and briefcase having the door marked "Hearing Room" held open for her by a guard and I say "Who's that lady there? Someone in the tribunal? The judge?''

"We don't have judges. She's today's hearing examiner, which might as well be the judge and jury so far as you're concerned, for her word's fact and law.''

"Ma'am?" I shout to the door.

"Please, she has her own full workload—she has to prepare.''

Examiner's stopped by the door and is looking at me. I run over to her.

"Ma'am? Hearing examiner? My name's Shaney Fleet. I know you're tied up but I own a bar and grill that's been closed. Here, look at this please and see if I don't rate something fairer —an earlier hearing today if you can make it," and I open the summons to show her.

"I am extremely busy, Mr. Fleet. Any dealings with the tribunal, see the clerk there.''

"I've seen her. She's been very nice but I can't wait any more days. Each is a dollar for me—many. I've no savings. I owe rent—home and bar—you can't imagine the bills. You shouldn't've shut me down if you have to put so many days between the shutdown and trial.''

"If the city gave us the funds we needed we'd see you the

same day you were shut down. And it wasn't the tribunal that closed you. It can help reopen you though and return your health permit if that's it, and it's a hearing you've been summoned to, not a trial. You were closed by the inspection arm of the department which, after two mandatory inspections, must have thought your establishment was a hazard to your customers' health.''

''What was such a hazard? Garbage bags in the basement that weren't picked up? He could've given me a hearing here first before closing me or a third inspection or just fined me without taking my business away for a week. And that garbage was downstairs, just a couple of days old and not even smelling, and the customers up.''

''Then you probably had exposed food near that garbage area and he asked you to remove the bags or make arrangements where they could be removed in the next day or two and you couldn't.''

''I couldn't because I've been honestly trying to get rid of those bags and can't.''

''That's presumably why he closed you then.''

''What if I tell you that he might've closed me because he's on the take from a private garbage company who besides doing other things to me are trying to drive me out of business?''

''I'd tell you that that's a very serious charge.''

''It's not a charge, just an idea.''

''If that inspector were here and heard you make that idea, he could charge you with libel and probably win easily if you couldn't prove your idea, because I'd be both his adviser and witness.''

''But he isn't here.''

''But I'm here and telling you to control yourself or else I'll bring you to court and charge you with libel in his or the Health Department's name and this office will be my witness.''

''I heard what this man said,'' the guard says, ''and I'd be willing to, Mrs. Fortiago, I would.''

''Sure you'd be willing to,'' I tell him, ''sure you would.

You're all such a bunch of damn robots for your positions and salaries—saying anything anyone higher up wants you to just to secure your jobs."

"You retract that or I'll institute a libel suit against you and use Mrs. Fortiago as my witness."

"I would for him too, Mr. Fleet, no matter how many wasted days I'd have to spend in court waiting to appear. Because you can't run around libeling people left and right and think they won't sue you."

"All right, I apologize to the health inspector through you. I also apologize to you and this officer too. And to the clerk over there. I apologize," I yell to her, "for whatever I said to you good or bad—no, just bad. Now," to Mrs. Fortiago, "isn't there something you can do to bring my hearing nearer to today?"

She takes my summons. "I accept your apology by the way," without looking up at me.

"I do too," the guard says.

Seems to read my summons through. "Believe me. Your hearing, probably because yours is a small operation and so might suffer undue financial distress, was actually scheduled sooner than if it were a bar owned by a large company, so be thankful for that."

"I am thankful. Thank you."

"And from what it says, you've had multiple garbage offenses lately, not only with us but the Sanitation Department and Police."

"Where's it say that?"

"These tiny code marks on the side here. Your inspector must have done a city computer readout on you and after it thought it wiser to use his discretionary emergency powers to close you down now."

"All right. Honesty's so far gotten me nowhere. But it's true those little marks, but I can explain all of them."

"Do that at your hearing Friday. If I'm the examiner that day I'll listen to you as I do with every violator: intently and sympathetically. We're hoping for the economic survival of this city as much as any department, so we're not out to vengefully close anyone down for good."

"No, I want you to listen now or at the very latest tomorrow in that room."

"If I am selected examiner on Friday, then try as I might to stop this prospect from happening, what you say today can always influence me emotionally and psychologically against you. So I advise you not to burn all—"

"But you get cancellations, don't you? The clerk told me so. Several a day, maybe more on Tuesdays, so slip me in. I'm confident I'll win no matter what you might carry inside against me."

"King. If Mr. Fleet isn't off this floor in one minute, call another officer and walk him to the street."

"You can do that with anyone you want to, right?" I say. "Like in some country without our laws against it, right?"

"If I'm badgered in the hallway and where all my hearings are delayed because of it, then that's also considered contempt of court. Believe me, I'm being lenient. I could have the cuffs put on you right now."

"All right. I'm sorry. I'll wait till Friday like you say and have a very nice day," and I take back my summons and leave.

I go to the bar and clean it up good. I find paint under the basement stairs and start painting the inside front door and end up doing most of the walls and some ceiling and then have to sand down the messier paint spots on the floor with steel wool and then stain and wax every inch of floor including the kitchen linoleum and washroom. I next clean and paint the washroom. That place wasn't half so bad as the rest but I like to see the walls and toilet and mirror and sink there shine. That's what I want for myself in other restaurants and bars or would if I went to them so that's what I want my customers to have too. Not that one in maybe the last ten thousand ever thanked me for it —paid me a compliment like "I really appreciate a clean seat and washbowl in there," or even "One thing I can always depend on here aside from your snide remarks and flat beer is a nice-smelling and -looking john." Maybe they think that'd be stupid to say, but I wouldn't mind hearing it.

All this takes me most of the next two days. I don't do it just to keep busy but to make the best use of my free time. My hopes are way up I'll be reopening right after the hearing, with according to what Mrs. Fortiago and the inspector said, just a moderate fine against me and final inspection set for a few weeks later. So maybe other people who never would come in before will come in now when they see the place looking so great and I can in the time before the final inspection make up for the money I lost. How I'll get rid of my garbage to keep my health permit I haven't figured out yet, but on that score I'm hopeful too. Maybe through something to do with the courts. Or from now on I'll use linen service instead of paper napkins and things and buy no plastic or glass throwaways except the liquor bottles I by law have to and get one of those dicing-up disposal units installed in my sink where I'll reduce my total garbage to just what I can carry out at night in two to three shopping bags and dump in my hotel's trash cans.

I also at the bar watch some late night television by myself and drink my own booze. Not that much drink because I don't like this new feeling of waking up slow and cranky when before it was mostly fast and bright and also with my stomach sour as it's been becoming and head like lead.

Every so often when I'm working or resting someone knocks on the window to be let in. If I don't know him or can't ignore his knocks, I wave him away. If I both know him and he insists with a "What's this, a business or one-man social club?" I open the door and without letting him past me say "Read the sign. They might even be watching me now." Most ask me to make an exception this once: "The next bar's three blocks away and it's ballbreaking cold out and I'll need a drink just to walk there and who draws a faster draft than you?" but I tell him I have to stay firm and for him not to take my no so personally. If he still urges me to I say "When you buy your bar you break the law the way you want, but I can't afford it anymore," and nudge him a little ways back onto the sidewalk so I don't catch his toes, and close the door.

During these days I also phone people who might know something about Stovin's illegal activities or were here when some of that business with his two goons went on. All say they can't be a witness for me and most think I'm crazy or wrong to have asked them. Comments like, most times followed by their hanging up: "Leave me out of it." "My heart couldn't take getting involved." "Breathe my name in this and you've lost a customer and friend for life." "I switched over to Stovin because I wanted to, not through force." "What are you talking about what two thugs? I wasn't there the day you say—you must've been seeing things or drunk." A few also say they're afraid for their lives and wives, kids, businesses, homes, jobs and cars "and if this phone talk's tapped or being taped," one of them says, "I deny or will I ever said any of this, though don't ask how I plan to get away with that."

So okay. I don't want to try and force them through the court to talk and because of me have someone's arm broken or lose them their livelihood. Besides, I've a strong feeling it'll all work out with no help from any of them through the ways I said: returnables, linen service, maybe a washer-dryer I can buy on time, and by hand getting rid of what garbage is left at night. There might even be, through a newspaper ad I can place but not one which Stovin's could know was put in by me, a builder or landfiller or even a sculptor or two who can use my broken-up liquor bottle chips and other trash for some industrial or artistic purpose or like that if let's say I brought it to them free once a week or where I might even get paid for it. Then maybe in a few months or year Stovin's will realize I'm not leaving and let me alone forever and I can get a regular carter to pick my garbage up. Ideas like these don't seem too farfetched and anyway they're just quick thoughts for now, not full. That'll all come after the hearing.

Day of the hearing I show up with my best clothes on and

shaved twice and hair slicked down and parted to make me look presentable and clean-cut. And my mouth mouthwashed bright and nothing harsh eaten anytime after so I don't stink from food or last night's booze and give any hints I'm the lush or slob I'm not. When I get off at the tribunal floor I show that same hearing clerk my summons. She looks at it and me and says "Yes, I remember the name. None of my business, but I hope you're a lot calmer for today's proceedings."

"Absolutely. I was just in a rotten mood then."

"Rotten mood you call it?"

"That's all. Series of things going bing bang bing really bad for me, but not my usual manner. How are you today?"

"Me? Same as usual."

"I guess that's good then."

"That's the same as the 'same as usual' is the same as usual then. I come in, sit, take the tirades as I did yours that day, have lunch breaks and clear my desk and leave and fight the subways home same as I do getting here. Take a seat and you'll be called when your turn comes."

"Thanks."

"Don't thank me. Think I'd be here if I had the choice not to?"

"Then tell you what. You take over my job and I'll take over yours."

"You'd have to study for and pass a rigorous civil service test that's even more rigorous today and then if you don't know anybody as I didn't, wait for an appointment for years. But I've work to do."

"I was only kidding anyway," and sit on a bench. Other restaurant and food store people wait around with me, some talking with lawyers. "I don't care what you swear happened," one lawyer says. "You'll tell them this, not that, but this, or I'm off your case, understand?" Several people are called one after the other once ten comes and an hour later the clerk calls my name and points to the hearing room and I say "Thank you," and smile at her and go in.

All that's in there with me is a court stenographer, different guard than from the other day and the same hearing examiner. I would've thought, once she saw my name, that she would've been fair and disqualified herself for another examiner. I say "How do you do, Mrs. Fortiago . . . sirs," to the stenographer and guard and she says "Hello, Mr. Fleet. Please be seated. This won't take long."

"That sounds like what my dentist always says."

"How's that?"

"That it won't take long. Then, two hours later . . . but I'm wasting your time."

"We can probably survive a little levity in here. What happens two hours later?"

"Well not 'always,' but he's still drilling and my mouth hurts like hell—excuse me—and I find I've lost a couple of teeth when he didn't tell me he'd yank them, few have been filled which is okay and I owe him four hundred dollars more than I can afford to—something like that."

"I hope that doesn't happen here. Incidentally, Mr. Fleet—"

"And not the whole teeth I didn't want to mean but the nerves. Root canal. That actually happened last year."

"Did you sue?" the guard says.

"I didn't want to get him in trouble."

"Oh, he can do you but you not him? I would have. They're supposed to let you know beforehand what they're taking out or minor surgery, not the reverse. It's in the medical ethics code, so probably dental as well."

"I also couldn't afford the time in court."

"For four hundred dollars plus damages you couldn't afford one day? Then you're making way more than me, brother."

"I guess I should've. I'm really not doing well at my bar."

"Incidentally," Mrs. Fortiago says, "if you prefer, because of what I said Tuesday about my emotions occasionally motivating my mind after I've been verbally assaulted, we can postpone this hearing till next week when there'll be a different examiner."

"If we postpone can I get my place opened till then?"

"Not till you've had your hearing."

"Just being here, showing I came when called and right on time, that doesn't count in my favor?"

"Perhaps with my decision later, but you still have to be heard first."

"Then it'd just be one more no-money week if I waited and I've no feelings you won't be anything but fair. But you know, I saw all those lawyers in the hall, so you think my chances here would be better with one?"

"Since your business isn't incorporated, no lawyer's required unless you wish to be represented."

"Then I'd have to postpone this for a few more days and pay through the nose for one. No, let's get it over with. Whatever wrong my summons says I did I'll go along with, because all I want to do's reopen."

I'm sworn in and she reads my Health Code violations. Refuse and rubbish stored in cellar. . . . No physical separation of food storage and cellar waste area in question. . . . Claiming to health inspector that previous day's garbage had been disposed of and then withdrawing that claim when offered contradictory evidence by inspector. "You've any defense against these violations?"

"Could you read them again?" Stenographer starts to. "No, forget it, because I'm only wasting all of your times now by saying I don't understand them when I do but am just trying to come up with much better reasons to defend myself. Because how far am I going to get by saying I've no proof and nobody to vouch for me here that this same gangster company I told you about Tuesday who wanted me to have my garbage picked up by them, then stopped me from having my garbage picked up by anybody when I refused them?"

"There were other ways to have your garbage removed."

"I know, and I knew that's what you'd say and I'm not denying these violations that I didn't do them. But I tried all those other ways to the point of getting my head bashed, apartment torched, arrested by the police, hundreds of bar dollars stolen and probably my business ruined and a huge fine heaped on me now by your department for these violations I can't defend and for lying to your inspector. And what did it all get me except your probably saying now that this denial of my rights to get my garbage removed and run a legitimate business isn't this tribunal's jurisdiction but one for the civil or criminal or whatever courts we have for this, all of who it'll also be of no use to go to, and that I'm still in violation of your Health Code, now isn't that so?"

"Is that your defense?"

"Yes. Those are them, what do I have that's better? Strong-arm stuff so nobody would do my pickup, etcetera. I must've left lots out, but how'll it help me? And everything I did to get rid of the trash worked in reverse to the point as I said of this long scar and metal plate in my head that I can show you." I bend over. "So how about just fining me what you have to, returning my health permit and letting me make a living again and thinking of ways to deal with my garbage problem so I won't have to come here anymore?"

"What your conflict with this private carter might mean to me personally *is* another matter. All the tribunal can be concerned with is if you presented a valid reason for operating in violation of the Health Code. You haven't, so I'll have to fine you"—her finger runs down a page—"three hundred and twenty-five dollars. I also—"

"Three twenty-five? I thought one twenty-five, one-fifty at the most. You'll have to lower it."

"You can appeal the fine and ruling. You'll still have to pay the fine to get your permit back today, but if you win the appeal, the fine or reduction of it will be refunded plus the minimum savings bank interest for the time we held it."

"Where will an appeal get me? No proof, so same business. Few people who feel for me and can speak with information about my case will run into the same trouble I did with this company if I used a subpoena to drag them here to talk, which they'd be too afraid to anyway. No, three-twenty-five's got to be okay, though how'd you reach that figure? Forget it. Just hope my check doesn't bounce, for that's how far into hock I am with this garbage, but thanks. Have a nice day. You too, gentlemen. Where do I pay—the clerk outside?''

"Not so fast. Your final inspection's in three weeks. Fail it and your place will be subject to being closed for a month. You'll have to show the inspector that your violations have been corrected and refuse is being removed regularly. Manage that any way you want to long as you get it out of there: by hand, van, dump, private carters of any criminal background or even burning it on the street if the smoke doesn't go in your bar and end up a health hazard to your customers and so a violation from us. I also suggest suing that carter if what you say about it is true—this is off the record, stenographer. If you win it'll have to reimburse you for your fines it was responsible for and probably pay heavy compensatory damages to you. I also wasn't serious about burning garbage on the street. That would only be another violation of a city statute, but one regulated by Sanitation, Fire or Police.''

"Don't worry. I know what to do with my trash now without making a fool of myself again, so it's going to be okay.''

"Fine. Goodbye.''

Guard hands me a slip to give to the clerk and opens the door for me. I write out a check for her, get back my health permit and keys and start for the elevator.

"That was stiffer than I thought it'd be,'' she says.

"What?''

"Nothing, nothing. I was calling the next customer. Eugene Smit? Mr. Smit?'' Man stands. I leave the building and go to my bar.

I phone a barowner I know and say "Know of a good cheap linen service?'' and he says "Who rents linens anymore?'' and I say "Not for me, it's for the son of a dear friend who's opening a bar not anywheres near us. But it's going to be much higher class than ours—the new look: stained glass—"

"That's new?"

"Then the new old look or old new. Hanging live plants and brown ceilings and walls and younger clientele—backgammon, fancy dried sunflowers in the shithole and stuff. He's got a few estimates but thinks they're steep and wants me to see if it's because he's new in the business he's being cheated much more than an oldtimer would."

"This dear friend or son of one isn't you by chance? Because you still have troubles with an unnamed company I won't name and want to cut down on your garbage bulk, wrong?"

"All right, it's me and you're right, that's why, but you know of a good cheap one?"

"I don't know if you heard but word's out you're bad news and even a worse troublemaker and nobody's supposed to touch you even by phone."

"Who told you that?"

"Skywriting. You can see it on any clear day."

"It's been snowing mostly and I never learnt to read skywriting. Who?"

"Then the stars in the sky one night when it didn't snow coming together to light up your name and reasons why, so just look up, it's there."

"Come on, let's see how gutsy you can be. Name names."

"Brains, not guts. And where you come off with this gutsy stuff when you lied to me about linen service for that son without caring one way what this unnamed company might do if they found I not only spoke to you but helped. Not that I know anything about them or could with linens for you, because if you ever find a service both good and cheap not to say dependable and I didn't in the future for now want to hear from you, let me know. For now, try the yellow pages."

I phone another barowner I know less well and say "I need a good cheap dependable linen service to cut down on my garbage bulk because of what you must've heard is my trouble with Stovin's and the Health Department."

"I don't know any service. But go to a phonebooth and tell the operator you're having a hard time dialing my number and could she personally dial me?" and hangs up.

I lock the bar, cross the street to the booth and tell the operator what he asked and she does her business and he picks up and she says "Linix Bar?" and he says "Yes, this from a public booth, Miss?" and she says "It is, here's your party," and he says "You off, operator?" and there's nothing and he says "That wasn't infallible but best I could do spur of the moment. Honestly, my heart bleeds a thousand miles for you, Shaney, but I always thought you were much smarter than this. What happened to you?"

"You went through all this to ask, then you know."

"I meant what happened to your smarts? In the past if I ever needed advice in this business I'd pick up the phone first to you. But with this garbage thing and an outfit like Stovin's and your not dealing in directly, something in you must have snapped. Hey—and I mean it and will always be your pal from way back —give me a ring when things stop sizzling for you," and hangs up.

I phone from a list of linen services in the yellow pages which advertise "lowest prices for restaurants and bars" and get estimates and they're much higher than I can afford. To the last, under Z, who gives me the one halfway reasonable estimate, I say "I won't go any further, I'll rent from you. I want to be straightforward also, since I don't want to lay any later headaches on you, so do you know of a Stovin's Carting Company?" and he says no.

"Really?" and he says "Really, and why should I? There are five million of them."

I tell him about Stovin's and why I need the linens and he says "Look, my theory in business like my father's in the same line was—"

"Yeah? Me too. Same place and my grandfather in it too."

"Terrific. Like me and both our pops, we're all good sons. But my theory is that your business is your business and mine's mine. Mine's to turn a profit and if yours isn't then that's your business too. But I can't turn without your business's business, got it?—so whatever problem you have with somebody else about business isn't my business at all. You're my business. You!''

"I just thought that this carter could be linked to linens or something, both of you in the restaurant business or part. So I just wanted to warn you—"

"What have I been saying?"

"I know. And I don't want to make a row now that you'll linen for me."

"What row? You couldn't, because I love you for your business. I love all my customers who pay. And that carter and us: you sound like you can take care of yourself, I can certainly take care of myself, so we struck oil together and let the rest of the world dig for piss. I'll deliver a bundle tomorrow and pick up and deliver twice a week after that. In two weeks I'll know how much you need and that's the amount you'll get weekly except for the big drinking holidays or if my linens start helping you double your trade. I'll need a week's deposit from you," and quotes it and I say "That's fairer than I figured."

"Maybe I should jack it up for you then so I don't look like a schmo."

"No, it's way above my means as it is, and thanks."

"Like I told you, bro, you're not on this earth to thank me, I'm here to thank you."

"Still, thanks."

I phone my beer distributor and tell him to send someone over to exchange my unused disposables for only returnables from now on. He says "Who has returnables? You want them, join the pro-deposit rally next month, which you'll see us there howling and maybe swinging against them, or move to another state."

"Then bill me for two kegs more of beer and one of ale a week of whatever you got me down for, because that's the only kind of brew my customers are going to get," and he says "Will do."

I phone my soda distributor and he says "I have no returnables nor does anyone in the city except for imported tonic and
bitter lemon that'll set you way back. What I'd do to avoid non-
returns is get one of those five-drink soda guns. It'll cost you a
pretty but in the long run you'll wind up a saver."

"What are the five? Soda, ginger, cola, tonic and what?"

"Water."

"Water I get out of my tap."

"So now you get it from the gun. It looks as if purified it
shoots so soft out and with no glass cloud and I swear also tastes
better in the mouth. I bet it raises the respect of your place and
so along with that the bar prices to people who love the fanci-
ness and gadgetry of it. I'll still send you the mixers but in big
drums the gun tubes are tied to and my cousin will set up and
sell the CO_2 and guns. You want two or three?"

"One."

"You need one for each bar side at least. Looks great with the
five tiny button lights and saves plenty of wear on the feet."

"One. I don't even see how I can pay for that."

"Don't speak to him of not paying, we'll worry about that
after it's in. I'll arrange things now and get back.-"

I tell my customers that if they want beer and soda in bottles
or cans they'll have to take the empty containers with them and
leave them somewhere outside but not in front. Most say they
don't want to lug any junk out and they'll have their drinks
straight or with water or peel or this time their beer or ale from
the tap. A few can live with getting rid of their empties, but
after they leave I find their bottles and cans on the bar or floor
or tables in back, probably because they're just too tired or lied
to me or aren't used to taking them from a bar so forgot.

That night I end up with two big plastic bags of garbage for
the day, put them in the basement with the others, get rid of
one of the smaller old ones by emptying it in four shopping bags
which I drop in different trash cans on my way to the night
deposit box and hotel.

"Phone message for you," the nightclerk says, "which I won't, if you don't want, relay."

"What'd they say this time: welcome back?"

"Practically that exactly, you're really onto their game. By the way. There's a new truly beautiful young lady who checked in today, so pretty and bright I don't even know why—"

"No, I already told you—yes, sure, send her to me please if she's not too steep."

"Never spoke about it with her so work it out yourself."

When she comes in my room I say "Lookit, I don't want to do anything, but have so much on my mind that I've got to spill it out to somebody who'll maybe only say something at the end if you like. So for the same amount you charge for the regular thing, I'll just talk."

"Thirty dollars is what I normally charge for twenty-five minutes, but for just talk, twenty minutes for twenty-five."

"I thought fifteen dollars for half an hour."

"Twenty-five and for a half hour. If you want I can also get undressed while you talk or play with you while I'm dressed and you talk. But for the twenty-five you don't touch me back either way unless you pay more."

"I don't want to be touched or played with, I only want to talk. It'll be more than half an hour also. Sit down, have a drink. Let's act like friends. Drink as much as you want to. Finish the bottle, I've another. I also have a couple of tasty meat and cheese sandwiches I made and brought from my bar and they're tonight's, one with mustard the other mayonnaise, but make it fifteen dollars tops for the half hour and five dollars for every ten minutes after that."

"Twenty-five dressed or undressed for forty minutes maximum and that has to be my lowest low."

"I'm sorry, I'm really short. I've bills up to here to pay beginning tomorrow which is just one of the things I wanted to talk about, so excuse me for bringing you here for nothing."

"That's all right, I don't mind having my time wasted by a bullshit artist," and she leaves and slams the door. I throw my glass of scotch after her. Minute later when I'm picking up the pieces the nightclerk calls saying "What are you doing to those gorgeous girls beside breaking down the hotel? I know you have problems but don't make me toss you out of here."

"If you want, give her a five for her trouble and add it to my bill."

"You come down here and give me that five plus two bucks for my efforts and keeping my mouth shut."

I go downstairs and give him a ten. "You know, my instincts were right the first night when I told myself I could never talk to you about anything half-deep inside," and walk away without waiting for my change.

"Because you gave me three dollars more than I asked for I won't say anything back."

Next morning there's a pile of garbage bags in front of my bar and Sanitation violation under the door. I call Sanitation and say "Those bags you ticketed me for aren't mine. Mine are in my basement—illegally—but that's Health's business, not yours."

"As I once said, anything on your sidewalk—gum wrapper, cigarette butt—is yours if we find you haven't swept it up."

"Where do you live?"

"What's that to you?"

"Because if I leave them in front of your house they're yours according to your laws, correct?"

"I live in a huge complex so I don't care where you leave them in front."

"Even if they piled right up to your fourteenth floor and stunk up your kid's bedroom?"

"That's just dumb."

"Anyway, you can't close me down. Only Health can do that, so I don't care how many tickets from you I get."

"You'll still have to pay them."

I put the bags between two parked cars across the street and go in my bar. An hour later one of the cars can't get out because of the bags and the driver sticks a few of them in front of the antique store where the car's stuck. The antique man runs out and argues with the driver, throws one of the bags at the car and it breaks and goes over and on the car and into the street. The driver jumps at him. There's no physical fight but almost one and a crowd forms and I can't see anything but hear screaming and when I open the door some people saying "Let him have it, Tim, give it to him." I'm watching this while serving drinks and making someone eggs and feeling bad I started the brawl. A police car comes, policeman gets out and stops the argument or fight and antique man goes in his store, bags stay outside and driver and police car drive away and crowd breaks up. Two other bags are still in the street by the curb where I put them and a minute later another car backs into the spot, runs over the bags and smashes them and parks with the broken bags and scattered garbage underneath. A little of it rolls and blows across the street to in front of my bar.

Few minutes later the phone rings and man says "Mr. Fleet? I'm Phil Veritianien from Bee's Antiquery across the street. I'm new in the area, probably paying four times your rent per-square-foot space, but want to keep the best relations with my fellow storeowners because we need each other for protection and eyes. But I never had a store in even the most wretched neighborhood where I got my lip slit and shirt ripped off my back and myself almost arrested for not telling the police where certain trash bags originally came from because I wanted to protect one of my fellow storeowners on the street. That the way you always dispose of your shit?"

"No and I'm sorry. I'll pay for the shirt and it won't happen again."

"I'll buy that offer. Thirty dollars. Since you're so tied up and my shop's always locked except for customers I sense I can trust, just slip it through the slot in my door."

I stick the money through his slot, then phone him a minute later and say "Don't know why I didn't think of this before, Mr. V. You couldn't take a few of those bags off my hands for a while every night if I stacked them nice and neat on your sidewalk at the right pickup time?"

"My carter only permits so many bags per day for what I pay, so afraid I can't, nor do I appreciate your asking."

I phone the soda distributor and he says "Take it easy. My cousin's out of town and should be back early next week."

"You wouldn't know anyone else who sells and installs them cheap?"

"Sure I know but if Vince heard I did he'd ask what kind of relatives are we for me not to give him first shot."

I call the linen service and tell the man who answers who I am and he says "Tough luck, Fleet, but the boss's wife says we can't take any new orders on for a long time if ever. Owner went to the hospital with a heart pain this morning and looks to be in bad shape."

"You know that's just crap. Who'd he speak to—Stovin's and they told him not to service me?"

"What do you mean?"

"You know what I mean. I mean your outfit for all your boss's big talk about his business is his and mine's mine and so forth was just a cover for—well is just like all the other businesses yours is in doing business with me and that's that Stovin's tells you who and not to sell to and you go along. I didn't explain myself well but you still have to know what I mean. Stovin's, that's who."

"Listen here, you fucker. Ned Rater is my boss and also my buddy for fifteen years and he's the best sonofabitch that ever lived and fairest boss anyone's ever worked for, so don't go slurring him again or I'll drive my truck straight through your store."

"Good, drive it. With bar linens, right into my place. Because that's what your boss promised for today: enough to last me a week, and then drive right in again to pick them up and deliver more."

"He's sick, can't you get that in your head? He had a heart condition working long and hard hours all his life for ingrates like you. He might probably die from it tonight because he was too damn good to be true, so lay off."

"What hospital?"

"Think I'd tell you?"

"Yes, tell me, I want to show the Attorney's office how Stovin's gets everyone in on it to dump me."

"A hospital, stupid, that's all. But if I see you anywhere near it and you tell me who you are, I'll break your face in with a pick."

I phone several hospitals and one says a Ned Rater was admitted today and is in intensive care. I chase my two customers out, lock up and cab to the hospital, get a pass downstairs by saying I'm his brother and get off at his floor. But I jump back in the elevator just before the door closes and ride down thinking what the hell am I doing here, where have my senses gone: have I so totally come apart where I think I'm the only one who can have miseries? The poor guy's sick. Get your head screwed back on. You don't want to see another man with a mask over his nose and piss in his bag and maybe his bawling wife asking who you are and I leave the hospital, get a double scotch at a bar on the block, say to the bartender "Have one on me or the price of a drink if you don't touch the stuff or aren't allowed, because I want to toast to Ned Rater—Ned Rater, everybody," I say holding my glass up to the other customers at the bar. "A heck of a guy, a great boss, a brave wonderful buddy, may he live in peace or just die peacefully, whichever thereof," and they drink with me, bartender sets down his water glass and takes the price of two drinks out of my money on the bar and drops half in his tip tray and other in the register, customers go back to their talking and I wipe my tears away, not knowing who I'm crying for or maybe both, him and me, and say to the bartender "He's in the hospital there, really a fantastic guy, kind of like my brother," and he says "Lost one myself this year plus a baby sister the last one, so I know how you feel," and we shake hands and I tell him I'm sorry for his own recent misfortunes and drink up and go to my bar.

"You'll drive people away with your new hours," a regular

says waiting at the door for me and I say "Nothing I could do. When a friend's sick you got to see him," and give him a free beer for his wait, for a few minutes think about what I think I'm about to do, call the soda distributor and say "Okay, no more lies. Tell me straight off whether you were told by Stovin's not to help me in any way," and he says "Where'd you get that? No." And I say "Come on, George, straight off, no lying, yes or no?" and he says "Didn't I just say it? No." And I say "George, goddammit, straight off, no more lies, don't be afraid I'll tell anyone for I won't, so yes or no, yes or no?" and he says "Okay. Yes, yes you're not going to get a soda gun from my cousin or anyone in town, new or used, or anything to help you from anyone in the state from now on from what I can tell. So you better just give up on your place, sell the bar if you're smart while you can still sell it, because you should've listened when you should've listened to them months ago. But no, you had to go make a perfect fool of yourself and risk the businesses of everyone who dealt with you and maybe your life, so goodbye already, will you? Goodbye and goodbye," and hangs up.

I call a couple of bar supply places and give my name and the bar's and say I want to order two soda guns. Both men I speak to say something like "We're out of stock. It might take a week, might take a month, but when we get them in I'll phone you."

I ask the regular at the bar to call "for an unopened bottle of vodka or your choice, this bar supply place and say you're Carl Frost of the Morning Dawn Pub—no, he'll look it up and see there's no bar name like that and know it's a phony call."

"I don't want to make any phony call. I only want to drink and avoid walking down sewer holes."

"For two bottles then. Here's the number and this time say you're Ivan Satty of the Hospital Balloon—that's a real place and I know has no soda guns because I was just there today—and that you want two soda guns installed and all the service that goes with it."

He calls and the man he speaks to takes down the Balloon's

144

address and says a salesman will be over by the end of the day to show him the different types of guns he can buy.

I get two bags of garbage from the basement, give the regular his two bottles and tell him to leave, lock up, cab to Stovin's with the bags and walk past two men scrubbing and hosing down a Stovin's garbage truck in the street and go in the building's front door and put the bags on the floor next to the receptionist at the desk who's the only person here and say "Jennifer if I can remember, yes? Or maybe she's at lunch or quit."

"What is it?"

"Then it is Jennifer?"

"Was when I arrived here. Who are you and what are these?" pointing to the bags. "Not that I can't tell by the smell. Phoo. Worked here long enough to know that those two are days old, three at the least, so even if you're a best friend of my boss and this is a private joke between you, march those things to the street. We'll get infested here and I'll get diseased."

"I'm Shaney Fleet."

"Glad to meet you, sweetie, but what's your name supposed to mean to me?"

"You don't remember our phonecalls a while ago? The great Shaney Fleet, the one who's all the problems?"

"Oh you, excuse me," and lifts the phone receiver, puts it back and says "What if I mentioned for your own benefit to also march right out of here? And you seem like a nice guy, so I'll take care of your bags, no charge."

"Tell Mr. Stovin senior I want to see him about these bags. They're a present from me."

"I know. You're going to throw them around, smear up the walls, make a big scene. But no matter how much you're hoping for it, you won't be beaten up and tossed out for doing what you intend to, just collared by the police. So go, don't make for yourself more trouble and also frighten my wits. You brought your bags in, I'll give you a receipt for them if you want, but this is it for the day, okay?"

About twenty feet to the rear's a glass-enclosed office with no one inside it before but now a big man walking back and forth, smoking a cigar, in a fancy dark suit, motioning hard to someone or people I can't see to the right of the glass.

"That Stovin senior?"

She turns around, looks at the office, back at me. "Just tell me if you have a bomb or gun. You do, warn me so I can get up if you let me and walk out of here to faint. Because I promised my momma never to hang around when—"

"I don't have weapons."

"Didn't think so, you don't look the type. No, that's not Stovin—Mr. senior or junior boy. Now scoot on out of here before whoever that is notices you."

"Where's senior then?"

"Not in today."

"Who's that then? The office door"—I stare at it—"says Mike Stovin senior."

"Don't make me press the buzzer. I have one under my foot. I press it three quick taps and the police will come in a flash. We've had trouble with disgruntled customers, which is why we have this summoning device. Hey!—" because I moved her foot.

"You've no buzzer." Man's still motioning his hand to someone I can't see. Maybe there's a mirror there he's for some reason practicing in front of. A speech or I don't know what. He puffs on his cigar, takes it out and looks for a place to drop the ash, facing me for the first time. Looks like Stovin would look. Little bush mustache, big aviator glasses, tall and powerful as if he hauled garbage cans for years before he got smart to start his own firm and doing the things he does to make a mint and along with it, because he wasn't working so hard anymore, gaining thirty to forty pounds. He sees me, drops the ash in an ashtray, fingers something on his desk and his voice comes over a speaker I can't see but is somewhere near us.

"Who's with you, Jenny?"

She shoves a pile of papers aside on her desk and says into the speaker that was underneath "He was just leaving, sir. Deliveryman got the wrong address."

"Mr. Stovin?" I yell before she takes her hand off the switch.

He was already bent back up and about to motion to the person or mirror or people I can't see when he leans over the desk and touches the switch and says "I'm not either of the Stovins, but what is it?"

"I'm Shaney Fleet, Mr. Stovin."

"Who's Shaney Fleet and stop addressing me as Mr. Stovin. Neither father or son would appreciate it."

"You know who I am and who you are too. I brought a present for you. Garbage bags, mine, something you always wanted from me or used to, as I thought you'd like to see what goodies you missed."

"We've plenty, so don't need more presents of them, thanks. And whatever your purpose is here, even if I can tell it's for mischief, would you please leave immediately or must I have Jenny phone the police?"

I grab a bag and run up to his office. He backs back scared. Two men appear behind the glass and a woman. Woman covers her face as if the garbage is coming through the glass at her. I throw it, bag breaks and garbage spatters over the glass, something hard in the bag cracks it and things run down the glass too. Liquid, ketchup, hamburger someone only half ate, and floor's a mess.

"The police, Jenny," he says into the speaker. I turn to her but she's gone. "The police, Beth," and the other woman goes for the phone on his desk. I run back and grab the other bag and run to his office with it. He tries locking the door but I get it open before he can lock it and push my way into the room when he tries pushing the door closed. The two men jump me from the side once I'm in. All three are now grappling with me, trying to force me down, woman's on the phone, while I'm holding the garbage bag, trying to break free and throw it at Stovin and ruin his suit and fill his face with trash and knock off his glasses and step on them. But they got my arms tight and I'm going down so before they get me to the ground I rip open

147

the bag from below and it spills out over our pants and shoes and bottoms of their jackets.

"You moron," Stovin shouts jumping away and slapping at the garbage on his clothes, while the men still hold me and Beth's on the phone.

"I got the police," she says. "What should I tell them?"

"No, let the bum go if he wants. Tell them it was a mistake but that you might call right back. And you," to me, "you leaving or do we really have to get them here and charge you with entering, battery, vandalism and the rest of those and sue you for my new suit and theirs and her dress?"

"I didn't get anything on me," she says.

"You were assaulted or almost. We too and that's enough for a lawsuit."

I'm being held down, one man pinning my arms, other sitting on my knees and holding down my feet. Around us is my garbage.

"Phone," I say. "I want them here so I can make a fuss and tell them you're a goddamn cheat and fraud."

"Police around here are my friends and know I'm none of those things. But I don't want to talk to you. I want to get rid of you and clean up this place. Sit on him till the police come. Beth, get them right over. I'll get a couple of the boys to make sure he stays down."

He leaves the room. The two men I saw sudsing the truck before come in and take the place of the two on top of me who get up and brush off their suits and shake their feet in the air. Flecks of whatever was on their shoes fly around. "I've got to change," one of them says.

"I didn't get it bad as you," the other says. "Mustard. I bet it stains. And what the hell's this red? —What is that," he asks me, "wine?"

I shake my head. The one who wanted to change, leaves. Police come. I'm allowed up. Policeman says "No charges are being made against you so just go. Come here again uninvited and no matter what charges aren't pressed, we'll take you in."

I brush myself off.

"Do that outside," one with the mustard says.

I start for the door, policemen right behind me walking me out. I want to grab a lamp and throw it somewhere but don't want to get clubbed.

"Will you thank Jennifer for me for being so nice?" I yell back.

"I'll thank your mother," one of the truckers says.

I leave, pass the cleaned garbage truck, start walking to my bar though it's a long way and it's cold and looks like snow. The police in their car follow me for a block and drive past and one waves and they make a right and when I get to the corner thinking I'll wave back, they're not there.

I tape a sign on my bar window saying "Tomorrow, big party, going away wake sort of, all day, blizzard or shine, so come one and all if you've been customers of mine anytime over the years or my father's or grandpa's and if you like bring your family and friends, good people welcome," and go to the hotel and get drunk in my room and sing songs I knew as a boy and haven't sung since when about young love and war and fall asleep and in my dream I'm in a room big as a mansion's biggest room, a baron's hall or whatever it's called, not where the people eat but meet after dinner and maybe have brandy and dance, hundred-fifty feet long, forty feet wide, and it's a bar with stools for a hundred drinkers and round oak tables in back for two hundred diners and great paintings and grand chandeliers all lit instead of my prints and fluorescent tubes and all my customers well dressed almost in tuxedo and evening gown clothes and the wood floors shiny like I could never get mine and wood walls as if just moistened with oil and no television set or butts and cocktail napkins on the floor or cough-making cigarette smoke and spit and everyone enjoying themselves and talkative though not raucous and throwing down dollars after dollars for their drinks and I'm behind the bar not so much pouring anymore as supervising a dozen bartenders to and I'm in a suit with a shirt and tie like Stovin's and also a vest and my hands in my pants pocket and watch fob chain across my chest.

Next day I sleep late and get to the bar around noon. There's about ten people waiting in front and one says "We thought you were joking about the party and would never show up. What do you mean by it, they tripled your rent so you're through?"

"Through as I'll ever be in this bar and probably also the business," and I open up and say "Help me bring the cases of beer and soda up from downstairs and put them in the icebox and refrigerator. I'll look after the liquor and try and make sandwiches, for as I forgot to say in my sign, you can have all you want of that too."

So my party begins. Weather cooperates by being milder. Some women help me out bagging the garbage and making sandwiches and boiling eggs. In an hour the bar's jammed. In two almost no more people can fit in and an hour later a policeman squeezes himself through to the bar I'm behind and says "This place is a firetrap if you let any more in. You'll have to admit them one at a time when someone leaves."

A man I never saw before but who says he used to come and pick his dad off the floor of my grandfather's bar years ago volunteers to be the doorman so long as he's constantly supplied with bitters and gin. I give him the bitters bottle and tumbler of ice with my best gin and promise he'll get more whenever he calls for it and he sits on a stool by the door and starts letting people out and in.

I don't hold back on the drinks but can't do as most people want me to and that's leave the bottles on the bar, as it's against the city's tavern law and I want the party to last till its natural end. When someone gets drunk or sick I tell a couple of men to put him in the back to rest or in a cab if he wants to go home or back to work and if he wants to tell his family he's on his way or to pick him up here, to use my phone.

Another policeman comes in and says "You know you're not permitted to serve alcohol to anyone intoxicated," and I say "Have I ever broken the law to you before? So give me a break on my last day and forget it this once. Have a drink yourself and sandwich or whatever you like on the house—scrambled eggs," and everybody around us joins in with me and says "Forget it, Nick," or "Officer, this is a once-in-a-lifetime bar party so have some fun and don't spoil it for everyone." He says "I guess once in my life I can try it if no one calls the precinct to confess my sins," and accepts a drink in a coffee mug and drinks it and another and two more policemen come in and one says "So this is where you are, Nick, we thought you were mugged," and they take off their hats and coats till only their regular flannel shirts show and drink from coffee mugs and eat too.

Someone has a radio and plays loud music and I dance though I can't dance with a young woman I never met and then with her little girl and next with the girl's rag doll and a couple of couples dance on the tables and a large group dances on the sidewalk. One man dances on the bar till I ask him off and then say to him "What the hell, dance all you want on it, step on hands, kick the beer mugs off. This is the end of the place anyway and we're all good sports here, so do what you want as long as your aim's true so no one gets hurt and it's in clean fun."

Three people fall to the floor drunk almost at once and are carried to the back and some men and a woman sleeping it off in back get awake and start drinking and singing up front again. By ten o'clock I run out of food to make sandwiches with and next run out of ice and eggs and keg beer and later out of liquor and ale and lots of people thank me and leave because there's almost no wine or bottled or canned beer left. Then there's nothing left and people pool their money and go out and bring back a case of liquor and ice and later someone borrows another drinker's car and drives back with cases of beer and ale. Then it's nearly three and getting close to closing time and I'm tired though for the last few hours haven't made anyone drinks but just walked around joking and reminiscing and I say "Goodnight everybody, it's been great. Best night of my life or almost and I love you one and all but you have to go." I get slapped on the back a lot and hugged and kissed which never happened here before and my hands shook till they hurt and cheeks pinched and several people push ones and fives and a ten in my shirts and pants pockets and say something like "I don't care if all this was supposed to be free, go take a holiday or get laid someplace or give it to charity on me."

One of the last ones leaving says "Why not make it an after-hours club for one night?" and I say "What's to lose and I'm getting back my third wind." I lock the door and pull down the shades and party goes on with what drinks we've left and old customers I haven't seen for weeks and were probably at other bars and maybe till now told by Stovin's or someone to stay away knock on my window and door and are let in. Other bartenders and owners also come by after their places close with more liquor and mixers and beer, even the ones who wouldn't help me against Stovin or said they'd never see or speak to me again till my trouble was over with him. I don't say anything to them about it. Past's past, I might need one of them for a job in the future if I stick in the same trade or later return to it, and they're really nice people with their own I suppose reasonable self-interests and almost none with my kind of bar background and fatherly business and why spoil the night with harsh words, so I just continue to gab, drink, laugh and dance.

Around five a policeman raps on the window and says "You'll have to close, Shaney. Neighbors have complained of the noise all morning. I stalled them because I heard some of our own boys were having a feast in here, but these people say they have to get a couple-hours sleep before they go to work."

I announce to the bar "It's definitely goodnight now, folks. Anyone wants to take the mugs or even the stools home as a memento or whatever you see except my coat, hat and boots, please do. I don't want anything here left."

A few take stools and mugs and ashtrays and someone lifts the cash register and says "Okay?" and I nod and he leaves with it calling it an antique. Couple of the better tables go and some of the cheap prints and working equipment and all the bar tools are pocketed by the bartenders and owners. Then everyone's gone and I look in back, see that someone fell asleep on the toilet seat and zipper him up and walk him to the street and give a cabby more than enough money to drive him home. Then it's absolutely quiet inside, nothing left to drink except a bottle of scotch I hid, and I start drinking it mixed with some fizzled out soda water and begin smashing up the place.

"Here's to you, Mr. Stovin and junior boy if you've been a bad boy too, a good belt to your jaws," and I toss an empty beer bottle at the bar mirror and both break. With a bat I smash the mirror to bits, few slivers of it getting in my hand and wrist but nothing great and hurl all the stools around till they split apart and turn over the tables and kick the legs loose and slash the chairs against the bar counter till I've nothing left but chair backs in my hands and rip the prints off the walls and tear the frames from the glass and break both of those too and pop the light globes and bulbs with a broom but keep one on in the rear and front and smash every glass, pitcher, mug, jar, dish and plate in the place, heaving whole stacks and shelves of them to the floor and slinging them against walls and across the room. I tip over the refrigerator and with a carving fork puncture its condenser tubes, pull the grill loose but put on back in working order because the gas starts to leak and I don't want the bar to explode, pull down the liquor cabinets that have been up for fifty years and with a table leg punch their smoked and etched glass in and drink while I'm doing all this and when the whole bar's wrecked or just about and I'm sweating faucets and exhausted I go outside with a few empty bottles and throw them through the window and door. I want to set fire to the inside but there are four floors upstairs, three just manufacturing lofts with no people in them this hour but top's a live-in serious artist and her cats.

But that's enough destruction and I leave the lights on and door open when I walk out. Some people are in front watching and a couple in a car have doubleparked outside the bar to watch too. Ones on the sidewalk step aside when I walk by though I say "Excuse me. . . . Pardon," to every other one of them because I don't want to seem dangerous or so insane where they'd be scared of me.

Second I step off the curb they run into the bar including the woman from the doubleparked car to I suppose look for things to drink and take and maybe break more. Phone's ringing from the booth across the street when I'm walking past, I bet for me but for what? I watch it ring, then quickly turn around to try and catch someone from one of the doorways or windows near my bar spying on me, then run to the middle of the street to look at the windows and doorways in the buildings behind the phonebooth. They're all closed and dark on both sides of the street and nobody's in the doorways. I run to the ringing booth, lift the receiver and say "Hello, hello?" but no one answers though the phone isn't dead. "Come on, someone's there," when I hear with the receiver still at my ear a police siren from somewhere not far off. Gets nearer and I hang up and a police car tears down the street and stops in front of the bar. Doubleparked car drives off with its trunk open and no passenger. People run out of the bar emptyhanded and some with a number of things. Two men carry out the entire cooking grill, woman with a five-gallon jar of mustard I didn't know was still there, man with a single dinner plate and several table legs but that's all he has.

"Drop all that," the policeman shouts getting out of his car, but they zigzag around him or like the men with the grill walk fast as they can the other way. "I said to drop everything you stole, folks, and I'll let you get on your way," when nobody's in sight anymore except the men with the grill. He goes in the bar. I start back to it to warn him about the gas leak from the grill's pipes, then think he'll smell and know what to do with it and there's a sign on the building's doorway saying A.I.R. on fifth floor, and head for a nearby diner I know from when I had early morning bar work to do that opens at six.

When I walk in the counterman says "Morning," and puts a

154

cup of black coffee in front of me though I didn't even make a sign for it.

"Thanks," and give my order of cereal, eggs, sausages and toast.

Place is full of workers with those paper printers' caps on their heads from the newspaper plant around here. Phone rings while the counterman's pushing my toast down again because I told him I like it a little burnt and he answers it, says "I'll see," looks around and says to me "You're the only one I don't recognize—you Shaney Fleet?"

"What I do now?"

"Nothing I know and make it fast. This isn't your personal answering service and my wife's home sick."

I go with my coffee to the end of the counter near the door and say into the phone "Don't tell me, let me guess."

"You didn't have to go as far as you did."

"Doesn't sound like my old pals Turner or Pete, so who is it? Stovin the man himself? The rolypoly ball of smelly cheese?"

"He'd never have anything to do with calling you directly and certainly not till daybreak if you were someone big. But he was very mad about yesterday. Not only was that a brand new suit never once cleaned, but I shouldn't be saying this to you—"

"Sure you should. He knows your every word."

"He knows I'm calling, but not to reveal all the little facts. You humiliated him something terrible in front of his men and those women and that's what really made him so mad."

"You one of those two dressier men?"

"That's not neither here nor there but I'm not."

"It's not and you can tell him I'm truly sorry, but is this why you called? To tell me he's mad? That's nothing news. He's also crazy and a big stiff and sonofabitch too."

"You know, I'm very close to him and you're angry, so I'll forget what you said and just say—"

"You his son then?"

"No, Junior's not around. Has his own personal problems.

But I'll just say that if I could hear it in your voice that you are truly sorry, that'd be good for you for me to report back. But you're not. Because you have no sympathy for anyone, that's why."

"Oh please."

"It's true. No sympathy for Mr. Stovin and what the poor guy has to go through. You don't know how hard he works and his health because of it and what kind of hours and seven days a week and upkeep and payroll to meet. He hasn't time for fools coming in ruining his clothes and garbaging his place. If you did know all that and what worries he has—work and Junior on down to his two youngest kids' top college allowances and his mother-in-law's terminal illness right now and his wife's depression over it and because of hers, his, you wouldn't have been so sloppy and rebellious to him, isn't that true?"

"I would've taken it into consideration as they say if he'd've taken my situation the same way."

"What did you lose? Nothing. Lousy apartment? You're better off. A parrot? Quack quack. So you got your head cracked. So you deserved it chasing and busting the bestfriend's head of your fellow inmate. And what expenses you have? You're a single man, always been, with no gambling derangement or women and only an occasional cheap whore. If you developed a drinking problem lately, what better business to be in for it? That bar, even with the extra garbage expenses, would have been way more than you needed for life."

"Hey, will you?" the counterman says setting down my hot cereal where I sat. "Hang up and eat. You're tying up the only phone and when another customer comes in, your stool's taking his place."

"Give me a little longer. —And phoneman, I'm sure you have no name but how'd you know I was here? I'm taking it so casually that you did, but I'm in a diner where nobody should be knowing me and you got me tagged minute after I walk in, just time enough to dial me. Wait, don't go away. —Keep my cereal warm," to the counterman. "This call's important, so whatever you do don't hang up. I'll pay for the wait and seat space and whatever else you think you deserve," and run outside. Just as I get there I see fifty feet away a man running toward the corner. "Don't worry," I yell, "I'm not going to run and jump you. Couldn't anyway. Even with your coat on and I'm coatless you're much too fast, so come on back and let's shake." He runs around the corner. I go back in, say to the counterman "Thanks a lot," and into the receiver "Still there?"

"Thanks for nothing," the counterman says when the man on the phone says "Here." "I was nice to hold it but say goodbye now." I give him two dollars from my shirt pocket and he says "That gives you just five minutes more."

"Just saw your spotter," I say on the phone. "That how you always did it? Quick little guy through my bar window or wherever I went to or you also used cars or from apartments across my street or spotters inside? Just curious and only wanted him to come in for coffee, no more cracked heads. Anyway, take him off. I'm through."

"We have no spotters. And about your being through, you could have hung in some more. You were getting to be fun. Not to be mean about it, we were all enjoying what you were putting up with so well and your spunk against us. Though we had a whole bag of tricks for you in the future, so you weren't by a long shot done yet."

"I can picture your last trick. Me cemented to the bottom of a cesspool."

"Don't be silly. But what I also have to find out and this is the most important of the call is what your plans are starting today?"

"None of your damn business."

"Okay, get all the curse words out of your system. Damn, piss, shit, fuck too. But what's it going to be? I hope not the old mistakes. Staying in the city?"

"Might."

"Want advice? Don't. Want even better advice? Don't. We

absolutely don't want you around, period period period. Not for two years at least. We, so the truth goes, want to make a complete show to that little private garbage collection world that you knew what was best for you after all and so cut out for good. Then after two years, come home. We won't complain. And you've worked hard all your life and when you were a kid for your father when you went to school both, so take a long vacation. Make believe you're also taking it for your dad and his old man too, who I bet between them never took a vacation once.''

"They didn't. And I have no money for vacations.''

"That's what I also meant about your going too far and didn't have to. Busting up your place, what did it get? Stupid. Should have sold what you could first. Then if you wanted to have fun, break what you couldn't give away for nothing and if that didn't do it, then also your landlord's bar window glass.''

"I wouldn't've made much if I did sell.''

"Would have been plenty enough to keep you going for a few months. By that time you would have thought of something, like an out-of-town job. But now you're broke, aren't you, or close, and you're not going to do anything but go to pot worrying about it.''

"I'll stay afloat and keep alive.''

"Oh listen to you, such big brave-boy talk. No, you'll drink a lot and then too much all day and night because you have no other interests and then shoot off your mouth endlessly about how you outdid us somehow instead of just quit your bar and left town. Not that we couldn't handle your boozed-up bragging. But more you make a fool of yourself shooting off, madder we can become if what you say or at least your attitude gets around. No, we want the whole show. Get out of town. Those two years. Leave tomorrow and if you have to say anything to anyone about why you left, say it was because we were too much for you after a while but that's all.''

"I have no money to go anywhere.''

"You've a little, so that's enough. As for your hotel, run out on it.''

''I don't want to run out. I want to pay for it and all my other debts.''

''You need a loan?''

''Think I'd take it?''

''Think we'd give it?''

''Sure you would, at interest rates I couldn't in a lifetime repay. That way you'd get me out of town and make a pile off me besides and maybe even have better reason to dump me if I didn't come up with the interest and balance in a few months.''

''We'd make nothing from you and do nothing too because we don't do those things to people and second of all because there'd never be a loan. You're one guy we don't trust. But what are you going to do starting today? I'm here to know.''

''Can't talk anymore. Seriously, this counterman's giving me the eyes like he wants me and his phone dead. It's no personal answering service he says he has.''

''Just whisper to him Porky why.''

''Why like in the question?''

''Like in the letter. But what's the difference, you'd only be saying it, so he'll know.''

''What's it mean?''

''That you would have known if you had let us serve you months ago. All sorts of wonderful fringes coming from us. But since you're on your way out of here anyway, I'll be a good guy and tell. Means he won't charge for what you eat and will let you talk long as you want on his phone free.''

''Maybe I want to pay for my meal and don't want to talk.''

''Then you're really stupid. Because who else is giving you a free meal when you're hungry and a phone for as long as you want, especially when you still have unfinished business to discuss? You can even call long distance when we hang up. Go on, tell him you want to call out of town and as far away as you like.''

''I have no one out of town. And what more we have to discuss?''

"Such as what I don't want to harp on again but you're forcing me to about your making it a big thing and sticking around the city and junk—just don't."

"I'll see."

"I said don't. Telling you, advising you. I'm actually going way beyond what I intended and befriending you: leave the city by this afternoon at the latest. But without talking to anybody about your bar, or at the most, if you have to, then that you were quietly forced to go. Or as a compromise, that it was over some woman you went crazy for and left—that always works and it'll build up your rep."

"Will you get off the phone?" the counterman says. "Your five minutes are long up and I just don't want you on anymore."

"Porky Y," I say.

"What's that again?" Comes closer, says low "Tell you what. This time use it all you want. Don't make it a habit, but use it now. That line about my wife is to keep the other slouches off because most can live on the phone. When you're done with your call I'll reburn you some new toast."

"The old will do. I like it both cold and burnt too. No kidding," when he puts another two pieces in the toaster, "I do. —That code message of yours really worked," I say on the phone. "About the other thing, I'll think it over, but I'm too sleepy and hungry to say yes now or no. Want to call me at the hotel later today or me call you someplace?"

"No. Answer now."

"Can't."

"I said your decision, Shaney. Last time: what's it to be?"

"Move to another city for so long? I don't know. I'm not trying to give you a tough time, but I never lived anywhere else. And about my mouth staying shut, how do I know all times what it's going to say?"

Hangs up. I sit down and the counterman gives me a fresh bowl of hot cereal. I mix in the milk and pat of butter and start eating. Phone rings. Counterman answers it and says "Yes . . .

160

Yes ... Yeah ... Sure." Hangs up, takes my bowl away though I'm not half finished with it, chucks it in the garbage pail under the counter while I eat off what's on my spoon. "Sorry, I can't serve you. You know what I'm talking about, so I'll see you."

"No, I don't know what you're talking about. I've money, so give me my eggs, toast and sausages and more coffee or I'm phoning the police from here and you can explain it to them."

"Don't make it hard on me. Just go."

"And don't hand me that don't-make-it-hard-on-me crap. Give me my food or I call from your phone."

"You can't use my phone."

Something catches my eye at the window. Man's behind it, ducks away. Seems like the one from before who also wore a dark suit and no hat. "Friend of yours?" pointing to the window.

"Who?"

"Sure, who. Mr. Peekaboo, I-see-you. I'll use your phone all right. I'll break your counter in if you don't let me and smash your window too."

"Please."

"No more pleases either. Some creep calls up, gives you the password on me like Porky T, Freaky E and says a fellow creep will be watching at the window what you do and that's supposed to be enough? Oh no, I've had it to here with them, so it also means with you. I want a new bowl of cereal, forget the spoon because I can use this one, and next my eggs turned over well-done and toast like I said and sausages and also a glass of milk. I want a cold glass of milk, all of which I'll pay for and the cereal one-and-a-half times for and because I'm an old bartender I'll leave a good tip."

"I can't. Now get out."

"What's the trouble, Irv?" a printer at the counter says. "Anything any of us can help you with?"

"No trouble," I say. "It's his business and mine and personal unless he wants to tell you just what it's about. Irv won't serve me because someone told him not to, that's all I'll say for now. Well screw Irv and you too if you butt in, because that's how I feel. I feel lousy, angry, scrappy, the whole thing of it, everything, up to here, that's how I feel. And I've money for what I want him to cook for me, so it's not like I'm trying to cheat the guy either," and I slap a five on the counter. "Now," to Irv, "you giving me my cereal and eggs or not?"

"Nothing."

"Then forget the police, what they do for me? And I'll make the food myself."

I go around the counter. Irv backs up all the way to the phone. Three printers stand up. "No," Irv says, "let him have his fun, just so he gets out of here eventually." Printers sit. I take a bowl off the shelf, plop a few serving spoons of cereal in from the pot, though I don't want anymore, look in the refrigerator for a piece of fruit, find a banana on top of it and slice the banana into the cereal and add milk and eat. I finish it and take the bowl around the counter, stick it with the dirty dishes, dribble some grease on the grill, crack two eggs and throw them on, turn them over, burn my toast the way I like it, pour myself some coffee and put the toast, eggs and butter on a plate.

"Forget the sausages," I say to Irv, "because I wouldn't't've been able to fit them in with all the cereal," and I sit and eat and drink. "The milk. Could you get me a cold glass of one?" He stands there staring at me. "I'm too tired to get up again. No, I'll get up, what am I making excuses for? Exercise will do me good and milk even better," and I go around and get a milk carton out of the refrigerator and pour a glass.

Phone rings. I look at the window. No one's there. Irv answers the phone and says "I know, I know. . . . Sure, on his way now," and hangs up.

"Them again?"

"No, my wife."

"Sure it is. She wants to know when I'm leaving. Tell her 'now.' How much?"

162

"Forget it I told you."

"That was just for the first cereal and single coffee."

"Don't bother. I can take the loss."

"The hell don't bother. This five dollars do you?" He nods. "Great. Here's another five for your trouble," taking it out of my shirt pocket and putting it on top of the other on the counter. "Really, I'm sorry for giving you such a tough time but you made me mad. I'm not that sorry though and I don't always act this way, but if I told you why you'd probably say you don't understand."

"Just get lost."

I put on my coat and hat and walk out.

"And don't do me any more favors with a return visit," he says when the door's shutting behind. I smile and wave at him. He gives me the curse sign with his hand. That man outside's not around and I walk to the hotel.

"Never seen you back so late," the nightclerk says.

"I'll be checking out later today, so get my bill ready for the dayclerk. Even if I can't pay it in full now, I'll get you the money in time and probably soon."

"I should ask you to leave right now with that sort of proposition you're offering, but you've had it rough enough lately so have a good sleep."

"I appreciate that."

"Hey, I'm not so bad and I'm feeling in a real generous mood today, maybe because of something good that happened to me. How about if I really got generous and sent you the new woman who checked in yesterday, compliments of me. She's up, I just saw her. All I'm asking is if you could phone me later tonight—"

"I won't be in the city."

"Then by phone from wherever you are, even collect to me if you're out of town, if she does it okay and was nice and sweet and no bitch. I heard bad words on her before she got here, and with me she'd only playact, so tell me this as a return favor and also, wherever you are to anyone, that I'm a nice guy."

"You're not worried about Stovin's?"

"Who's they?"

"Come on."

"Hey, this is another part of town, so he can't bother with us and we don't with him."

"Maybe he's just trying to make sure through you I'm gone."

"Believe me, I'm telling the truth, and your attitude the way to treat a gift?"

I go upstairs. Half-hour later when I'm tired of waiting and in bed and shade down and lights out thinking he was just pretending or had second thoughts about it because of all the money I owe the hotel or he got a call or whatever the case, someone knocks on my door. It's her, she comes in, says hello, shakes my hand, looks around, says "This room is a lot nicer than mine. Maybe after you leave I'll get it. Mind if I?" and I say "Sure," and she undresses, is very pretty and has a beautiful body and young.

"Eric told you," I say, "though I know it's a little late to say this if he didn't, that I don't have the money to pay you, it's all on him."

"That was clear, don't worry. Just move over so I can get in bed."

We make love and for me at least it's the best in my life, not so much the thrills but just nice. She isn't hard, she smiles but it seems sincerely, says warm things and kisses as if she means it and she doesn't seem dumb, she seems smart and is very clean. After it's over I say "Excuse me," go to the bathroom for a glass of water and she says "I hope you don't smoke, for that's the one thing I can't take. By the way," when I get back, "you were really great. I didn't feel like you were just anyone, maybe because you're not paying."

"I know you're only lying but that's all right, I like to hear it."

"No I'm not. Why would I?"

"Lots of reasons. And so what if you are. I said it's all right."

"You don't want to believe me, don't. Okay: you were the world's worst," and laughs.

"I'm sorry I said it then. You want a glass of water or something? A warm beer? Scotch?"

"No thanks."

"Then I guess you want to go."

"Eric didn't tell you? He said for me to spend the whole morning if you wanted, also on him."

"No, it's all right." When she gets up and starts dressing, I say "What am I talking about? Of course I want you to stay."

"Good."

I go to the bathroom for more water, come back to bed. She plays with me again and I try and almost do it but can't and I say "Maybe I'm tired, which I should be, or just not used to it so much all in so short a time in one day," and she says "That's okay, you wouldn't be the first. Goodnight."

I shut the light and kiss her and she kisses me back and we hold one another right into sleep. When I awake around noon she's gone. I jump up, look at the sun, punch the pillow and say "Good, great day, I'm going to stay."